RYANN FLETCHER

Exiled Advocate

Cover art by indy @strooooble

First edition

ISBN: 978-1-7393585-5-6

This book was professionally typeset on Reedsy.
Find out more at reedsy.com

Contents

Chapter One

She raced down the crystal-paved path towards the lake, face held to the sun as she shrieked with excitement. Stark birch trees rose up out of the earth, their foliage thick and verdant in the warm summer sun. She had everything she could ever wish for, and in that moment, she was the happiest she would ever be.

"Shailagh!" her mother called, smiling broadly with her arms held wide, beckoning her down to the water. "Would you believe that it's the perfect temperature?"

"Coming!" she squealed, tearing past an errant bramble bush. The delicate silk of her silvery dress caught on a thorn, rending apart each shining thread with the quiet yet insistent snap of permanence. Panic began to rise in her chest as she grasped at it, trying to hide the tear in her clutched fist.

"Shailagh!" her father shouted, grabbing her by the hand. "What have I told you about running like that? It's not befitting of a princess. It's not befitting of royal lineage."

"Faarys, she's just a child," her mother chided, standing up. She straightened her own dress, moving to smooth out the wrinkles. "Royal or not, she deserves to have some fun." She approached, resting a hand on his arm. "It's only fabric, dearest."

"The finest fabric in either realm," he replied sternly. "Child or no, she needs to learn how to hold her place in Fae court. She's old enough to start understanding the consequences of her actions."

She stared up at her parents, flinching away from the growing tension between them. It wasn't the first argument they'd had about her, and it was difficult not to feel responsible. Pulling from his grasp, she broke free and ran to the water, kneeling on the edge to stare into the glassy, mirrored surface.

At first, it was just her face that stared back at her, young and childlike and innocent. Her parents, rushing to catch up with her, one concerned, one furious. The crisp teal water rippled, disturbing the picture before her. The earth shook, and the lake boiled, disappearing into the deep chasm that had appeared at the center. In its place, a viscous purple sludge oozed up from beneath, pushing aside the land as if it were made of spun sugar.

The forest disintegrated one giant tree at a time, their limbs floating and carried away by the current. She tried to run, but she was rooted to the ground. She reached for her mother first, but she was no longer there. She reached for her father, who stared down from his safety on the bank.

Screams echoed through the ruined woods at the exact moment that the crystalline sparkling path erupted, shooting streams of purple magma into the air with unrepentant fervor. Pain, suffering, exposure.

She held her dress in her hands, and when she looked down at the ruined fabric, it, too, began to melt through her fingers, the purple fluid burning her skin and drawing ripe blisters to the surface. When she reached out, there was nothing there.

Birch trees swayed in the chaos, their roots twisting up out of the ground like tentacles, the wood far too brittle to bend. Bark splintered, the echo of annihilation like barbed thunder in her ears as one trunk after another cracked into fragments, the snap, crack,

thwack of files against a worn wood table. "Your Honor." Sadie took a breath, and exhaled it quietly. "As much as it pains me to miss the opportunity to spar with the prosecution, we all have to admit that there just isn't enough evidence for them to bring a case against my client."

The prosecution pointed across the table in accusation. His oversized, ill-fitting suit hung off him, nothing more than a mess of navy pinstripes and white pocket squares. "What Ms. Sinclair seems to be forgetting is that the prosecution had *plenty* of evidence, the cornerstone of which was our eyewitness to her client's crime of insurance fraud!" He sighed angrily, letting his arms flop back to his sides. "Your Honor, I humbly request an audience in chambers to discuss the possibility that Ms. Sinclair engaged in witness tampering."

"Your *Honor*!" she protested, gasping audibly, the hard intake of breath echoing around the courtroom and settling in the empty gallery seats. "I am appalled that Mr. Link of the prosecution would accuse me of something quite so unethical, not to mention *illegal*, in open court." She tugged at the hem of her aubergine suit jacket and flipped a dark curl over her shoulder.

The judge picked up his gavel, turning it around in his hands as he considered. "Mr. Link, are you prepared to offer evidence that the defense engaged in witness tampering?" he asked.

"No, Your Honor, we've yet to uncover hard evidence, but given her track record—"

Sadie spat out a laugh. "My track record?" she repeated. "Please, Mr. Link, point me to even one shred of evidence that I've done anything beyond the scope of the law, and I will immediately turn over this case to another attorney." She glanced at the door, the huge wood panels still closed, even as the minutes ticked by on the clock that hung above them. She cleared her throat and turned back to the judge. "Your Honor, I am simply asking for this case to be dismissed, as the prosecution no longer knows the whereabouts of their eyewitness. That's all."

Edward Link offered her an oily smile over the gap between their tables. "Your Honor, the prosecution asks for a continuance, in order to regroup and issue a subpoena to our errant witness. We are still prepared to question her, even if she has decided to be a hostile witness."

"Ms. Sinclair, I am inclined to side with the prosecution," Judge Haber said, clearing his throat with a wet sound. "They have indicated that there may be more evidence to support their claims, even if their witness declined to show up to court."

Hinges creaked open and Sadie had to resist the urge to spin around, triumphant, instead of waiting until Ella tapped her on the shoulder.

"Ms. Sinclair," Ella said in a loud whisper that could still be heard across the court, "I think you should see this." She looked perfect in a sapphire blue dress that skimmed over her shapely hips, her dark brunette hair shiny even in the dark courtroom, braided into an intricate crown around her head.

"Thank you, Ms. Beaufort," Sadie said, taking the envelope. She opened the flap and looked inside, feeling every eye in the court on her. The page read exactly as she knew it would, having prepared it that morning. Evidence, hidden by the prosecution that implicated another perpetrator that had long since fled the country. She raised an eyebrow, looking across to the prosecution. "How very interesting," she said evenly.

Edward flinched, shuffling through his paperwork noisily. He dropped a page, and it fluttered silently to the floor, coming to a rest under his polished patent leather shoe. "Your Honor, I would like to respectfully request a recess," he announced. "Just a brief one, if you will. The prosecution doesn't wish to waste the court's time."

Judge Haber considered the request before nodding. "Fifteen minutes," he said, smacking the gavel against its platform.

"What do you have?" Edward Link demanded, reaching for the envelope. Sadie snatched it out of his grasp, sitting back down in her chair.

"What do you think I have?" she asked. "Come on, Ed, you can't be serious with this case. You've got nothing, and this envelope proves that your office has been—"

He bent down, his face inches from hers. "Keep your voice down, alright?" he hissed. "Now, what do you want?"

Sadie glanced over at her client, a thin, weedy-looking man hunched over the table, still looking as terrified as a wounded gazelle on the plains, waiting for a hyena to finish him off. "Probation," she said. "Six months."

"A year and he has to pay a fine," Ed challenged. "Come on, Sadie, you know I can't go lower than that or I'll be on the chopping block next week." He pulled at his red silk tie, standing up straight again. "Or, we meet the judge in chambers, and I tell him everything I learned about how you employed the enforcer who scared off our witness."

"Do you have proof of that?" Sadie asked. "Because if not, it's nothing more than conjecture. You're grasping at straws, counselor. You and I both know I did not engage in witness tampering." She smiled up at him, clutching the envelope to her chest. "If you want the fine, then no probation."

"Six months probation and a fine, and that's the best I can do," he said. "And don't think I won't be watching you all the more closely next time we face off in court, Ms. Sinclair." Edward huffed out an angry sigh, irritated that he'd let a sure-thing case slip through his fingers. "Take the deal, you're not going to get a better one. Your client is in dire straits. Neither of us wants this to continue in court."

"Deal," she agreed, extending her hand to shake his. "We're ready to sign." She shuffled through her folders, locating the one with the green tab poking out of the side where Ella had placed it. "Fortunately, I already have it drawn up."

Ed narrowed his eyes. "Oh yes, fortunate," he deadpanned. "What a completely unforeseen scenario." He took a pen from his inside pocket, signing each page and dating it after he skimmed through the wording. "Tell your client to keep his nose clean or we'll be back in this courtroom in six months, and next time I'll make sure that he does time."

"Pleasure doing business with you," Sadie said, leaning back in her chair. "Anything good coming up next on your docket?"

"Why, so you can undermine that case, too?" he retorted. "All you shadows-damned ambulance chasers—"

Sadie interrupted him with a theatrical gasp. "Mr. Link!" she protested, folding her hands atop the table. "I've never once chased an ambulance, nor do I make it my business to scrape cases off the public defender's floor. Working on contingency certainly won't pay the rent, now will it?" She crossed one leg over the other, sliding the contract to her client along with the pen, already bleeding black ink into the margins of the first page. "We are supposed to be professional peers, not adversaries. After all, we all have to attend the same dry galas, don't we?"

"I happen to enjoy the galas," he said politely, taking the signed contract from her client and closing it into a folder. "As does my wife. It's an opportunity for the women to get out of the house and get gussied up." He shifted, staring a little too hard. "Perhaps I will see you there, if you aren't busy undermining more of my witness prep."

"I'll try to make time for it," Sadie said easily, ignoring the latter half of his statement. "Judge Haber, I think the defense and the prosecution have reached an agreement," she said, standing again. "I believe Mr. Link has the completed contract."

"Excellent," the judge said, taking the folder from Ed. He settled a pair of wire-frame glasses on his nose, reading over the contracts and nodding. "This all looks appropriate," he said, signing his name on the final page. "Ms. Sinclair, your client is free to go, but will need to stop at the probation office on the way out of the building."

"Thank you, Your Honor," Sadie said politely. The jury began to shuffle out, grumbling to one another no doubt about their wasted time and Sadie couldn't blame them. She hated her time to be wasted, too. "Mr. Pender, you will need to be assigned a parole officer, do you understand?"

Her client nodded, wringing his hands in his lap.

"My payment terms are thirty days," she reminded him. "And you will need to pay the court's fine, there's no getting around that." She nodded towards the door, and he silently followed her instruction, disappearing through the doors along with the rest of the jury.

Sadie turned in her chair, leaning over the divider that separated the attorney desks from the court gallery. "Nice timing," she whispered to Ella. "I wondered for a moment if you'd forgotten."

"Who, me?" Ella asked, batting her eyelashes. "Never."

"That last-minute evidence tactic is going to run out of steam now, at least with Ed Link. That man is out to get me. He *hates* me."

Ella shrugged, playing with the pearl stud in her ear, dainty and polite in its size. "He only hates you because you beat him." She crossed her legs, showing off shapely calves and a pair of blue t-strap heels that matched her dress. "And if that's the problem, I imagine most of the state's attorney's office hates you."

"Yes, it makes these galas rather uncomfortable." Sadie cast a sideways glance at Ella, wondering if it was worth roping her into it. If nothing else, she'd look amazing, just as she always did. "You wouldn't want to come with me, would you?" she offered, looking back towards the door to make sure her client didn't pass up the probation office on his way out. She'd almost been surprised he'd shown up to the court date at all. He'd made it clear that he preferred the idea of following his ex-friend out of the country to exile, but she'd convinced him to stay and clear his name.

"Oh, I can't," Ella apologized, biting her lip. "Ray is taking me to The Saffron Rose tonight."

"Of course," Sadie said, waving her away while internally roiling with poisonous envy. "I forgot. Your anniversary, right?"

Ella nodded. "One year this weekend!" She smoothed her skirt, plucking an errant thread from the hem. "You have that meeting tomorrow," she said, leaning in close. "Astrid Frost."

Sadie stifled a noise of irritation, aware that Ed was still watching her. "My favorite client," she said. "Her account pays the bills, I'm afraid, but it makes up for her perfectly repulsive attitude." She cleared her throat, watching Ed cross the courtroom once more. "What was it she wanted, again?"

"She thinks she has a squealer in her club."

"I can't imagine why she might require my services, then. Ella, do me a favor, call her when you're back at the office, and tell her to call Ms. Vane for this."

Ella nodded, standing up from the worn wooden bench. "Of course." She laid a hand on top of Sadie's, smiling. "I'm awfully sorry I can't come tonight. I hope it's not too terrible on your own."

"I will likely survive it," Sadie said, feeling like she should wave her off, but being completely unable to move her hand from where it was under Ella's. "It serves me right for being so perilously single all the time."

"Oh, Sadie," Ella sighed. "You'll meet that special guy soon enough, I just know it."

"Perhaps," Sadie said, staring, and she was distracted just long enough for Ed Link to snatch the empty envelope from her table. "Excuse me, Ed," she said, standing to snatch it back, "that's confidential."

"Oh really?" he said, holding it out of her reach, utilizing his tall, wiry frame to his advantage. "Something from my own investigation is confidential?"

"My case strategy certainly is," she said. "If you wanted to know what additional evidence I had, you should have pressed the issue before we signed a deal." She stood, aiming to match his height but falling short by about six inches. She reached for it, breath constricted in her chest, but he stepped backward, pulling at the lip of the envelope.

He held it upside-down and took the page, reading it with bewilderment. Ed looked back at her, fury collecting in the shallow lines on his face. "How did you get this?" he whispered, and the softness of the realization was far more threatening than any raised voice would have been. "You used pitted evidence?" Ed asked, still staring at the envelope. "How many times have you gotten your hands on something like this?" he demanded. "Who do you know in the state's attorney's office?"

"Ed, you and I both know that this never should have happened," Sadie said carefully. She took the envelope, slid it between her other files, and handed it to Ella over the barrier. "Do you mind taking these back to the office?" she asked.

"Of course," Ella said, keeping things short and sweet because she wasn't just one of the most beautiful women in Verdance, she was whip-smart and had saved cases more times than Sadie could count. Before Ed knew what was happening, Ella was out of the courtroom and rushing to flag down a cab from the front of the building.

"I'm taking this to Judge Haber," Ed declared, crowing it loudly, full-voiced as if he had a leg to stand on. "You manipulated this trial, Sadie. That would never have been allowed into evidence."

"Please, I encourage you to take this to him," Sadie replied easily, leaning back against the barrier because it was easier than staring up at Ed's narrow face, cheeks red and blotchy from the barely contained rage. She smiled at him, being sure to show all of her teeth. She'd had the second set of canines filed down years back, but the slight point was sometimes enough to cow people who weren't observant enough to realize why she was as unsettling as she was. "I'm sure the judge would love to hear about how you didn't do your due diligence before presenting a plea bargain."

"You should be disbarred," he growled. "You're an embarrassment to the law."

Sadie straightened herself to her full height, albeit petite in stature. "Mr.

Link, I have done nothing that would merit being disbarred. I received new evidence that may or may not have been admitted into the trial, but before you could ascertain the veracity of the documents, you panicked." She tilted her chin upwards, glancing at the mirror just at the edge of her periphery. "You may want to discern why it is that you felt like that was the best option." Standing with every ounce of her tarnished regal expectations, she adjusted the placement of the briefcase handle in her grip. "I hope to see you at the gala later."

Chapter Two

Sadie twisted the chain of her necklace, pushing the clasp to the back of her neck. She hated dressing up for galas, all satin and taffeta with uncomfortable shoes but it was the best way to hobnob with the legal elite in Verdance—even if she had to do it with three burgeoning blisters gathering on the back of her right heel. Human realm fashion couldn't even begin to compare with what she'd grown up with, Fae silk that whispered like secrets against skin and shoes made to measure by cobblers who had trained for hundreds of years. She sighed, doing her best to ignore the insistent press of the seams against her sides.

The venue was stunning but repetitive, and it had nothing on the courts from back home. A chandelier sparkled over the marble floors, and gold-painted railings wound up the staircases that flanked the main doors to the ballroom, with the soft glow of one single candle on each pre-assigned table. With any luck, she wouldn't wind up anywhere near Ed Link.

"Ms. Sinclair, what a surprise," said Judge Liesse, clasping her beaded clutch under her arm. "I always enjoy seeing who shows up to these things, don't you?"

"Absolutely, Your Honor," Sadie replied, blinking against the near-blinding array of reflections from the glass beads on the judge's dress. "I was here last year, though, and the year before that."

"Oh, of course, my mistake," the judge said, offering a surprisingly warm smile. "I wouldn't have thought a firm as small as yours would be able to afford a table at something like this." She plucked a flier from the side table, her eyes roving over the bold typeface. "Ah, another charity for the public defense fund. A worthy cause, don't you think?"

Sadie adjusted the teal satin gathered at her shoulder, wishing she'd ignored the dress code and worn something else, instead. "Yes, Your Honor, I would agree." The reflection of the door caught her eye, as well as the woman walking through it. Tall and elegant, the silvery fabric brushed against tile as it trailed behind her. "And yes, I practice alone. A few of us pool our funds to purchase a table."

"Have you ever thought about joining a real firm?" Judge Liesse asked. "My apologies, a larger firm."

"Oh, I think we do just fine on our own," Sadie replied, her tone sharper than she might have liked. "We secured a good deal for a client earlier today, in fact."

The woman in silver lingered at the matching table on the other side of the foyer, trailing a finger across the frosted glass. "I don't work well with others," Sadie added, turning her attention back to the judge.

"Yes, so I've heard." The judge leaned in, an eyebrow raised. "Between you and I, Ms. Sinclair, it would behoove you to practice playing nice, before you amass a battalion ready to lay siege to you." She stepped back, smiling again, except this time there was a flash of something resembling a warning that gathered in the corners of her eyes. "It pays to observe the social expectations," she added.

"I'll make sure to tell the prosecutors that," Sadie replied, her voice once again smooth and even, without even the slightest hint of a blemish brought on by embarrassment. "After all, they are the ones who frequently dislike the idea of playing nice."

"Good evening, what a delight to see you here," the woman in silver said, and for a second, Sadie was confused. She couldn't possibly be talking to her, yet there she stood over the judge's shoulder, beaming.

"Indeed," Sadie replied. "A wonderful surprise."

"I'll see you in there," Judge Liesse said, excusing herself to jangle into the gala, the thousands of beads on her champagne-colored dress dragging the fabric down in the back, marring the line of the cut.

The woman in silver arched one perfect eyebrow over thick eyelashes, her red lips poised in a friendly, if challenging, smirk. "You looked like you needed an escape hatch," she said. "All work and no play."

"I was hoping she wouldn't notice me," Sadie replied, laughing. "No such luck."

"In that dress?" the woman asked, leaning in so that she was almost towering over her. "I don't think anyone could keep from noticing you."

Sadie blinked three times, urging herself to come up with something, anything, other than stunned silence. "Thank you," she finally managed. "You aren't so bad yourself, Ms...?"

"Call me Clem," she said. "And you're Sadie Sinclair?"

"I feel like I'm at a loss here, given you apparently know me, and yet I don't know you," Sadie challenged gently. "How is that?"

Clem waved an elegant hand, the bracelet on her wrist catching the light and reflecting prisms onto the dark wall behind the table. "Your reputation precedes you."

"How ominous."

"Nothing bad, I assure you," Clem replied. "Only that you are rather formidable in the courtroom, Ms. Sinclair. A real force to be reckoned with, from what I hear. A thorn in the side of the State's Attorney."

"I presume any defense attorney tends to be a nuisance as far as he is concerned," Sadie added, keeping her voice to a hush as two prosecutors bustled past them, taking fliers as they went. "I'm sure he'd much rather be able to convict whomever had the bad fortune to wander through his courthouse." She leaned against the table, briefly checking her reflection in the window, pulling a chestnut-colored bushy curl back over the top of her left ear. As ever, the edges of the glass almost hummed with an iridescence, visible only to her. To her knowledge, mirrors were the only items in the human realm that recognized the Fae in her marrow.

"I've never seen you at the courthouse," she mused.

"Contract law," Clem answered with a shrug, the silver satin gathering over her skin, deeply tanned, and then relaxing back into place. "I don't have much occasion to be at the courthouse. And between you and me, I'd prefer to keep it that way. I hate having to make inroads at these events. I prefer to be unknowable."

"Take care, Clem, the singleton sharks will smell blood in the water." Sadie bit her lip, and then released it, surprised that she was flirting with a total stranger. "I just mean, it's not unheard of for people to get a little out of control at these things."

"Why do you think I'm here?" Clem asked with a wink, gracefully sweeping across the floor until she was at the double doors. "I think the opening ceremony is about to start, Ms. Sinclair."

Sadie followed, unable to resist looking back at her reflection once more. The pull back towards the Fae realm was almost impossible to resist, even if it would mean disaster and death for her to return. The jazz combo struck a loud chord, drawing the attention of the room. The speaker was Harold Evens, the lead defense attorney for Evens and Novae, the top law firm in Verdance. He tapped the microphone, clearing his throat.

"Good evening, everyone, and may I issue you all with a warm welcome to the annual public defense fundraiser gala. May I remind you that this is a charity function, so please open those pocketbooks nice and wide for us tonight."

"Hmm," Clem murmured, drawing her finger over the seating chart. "I've always found these to be more of a guideline, haven't you?" She swapped around two of the name tags, inserting her own next to Sadie's. "There we go, that's better."

Sadie would ordinarily have bristled at the rejection of gala etiquette, but there was something about Clem that invited intrigue and not irritation. "Ergh," she intoned with hesitation, unable to stifle the frustrated noise in her throat at seeing Ed Link's name at the table next to her own.

"What's the matter?" Clem asked, taking two champagne flutes from a passing waiter and handing one to Sadie. "Trouble with another attorney?"

"I faced Edward Link today," Sadie explained. "I don't think he'll be very happy to see me."

"Oh, I wouldn't worry about Ed," Clem said casually. "I don't think he'll be coming tonight. He was at my firm for a deposition, you see, and he was looking a little peaky after court this afternoon." She sipped at her champagne, leaving the hint of a lip print along the rim of the glass. "What did you do to him?"

"Nothing beyond the usual," Sadie said, not wanting to linger on her methodology. "I don't think he likes losing."

"That he doesn't," Clem agreed. "Especially not to small, single-lawyer firms like yours."

Sadie nodded. "Ah. So that is why my reputation preceded me?"

"He's mentioned you once or twice." Clem clinked her glass against Sadie's, her mouth set in a conspiratorial smile. "Keep on him, Ms. Sinclair. He'd never admit it, but he loves the challenge." She nodded towards the stage, a spotlight still trained on Harold Evens as the jazz combo vamped quietly beneath his speech. "What do you think of this old windbag?"

"Oh, I think he's a perfect example of an overly verbose attorney," Sadie replied. "But a powerful one, so we all have to pay our dues and do our best not to annoy him."

Clem threw her head back in a laugh, drawing the attention of several tables towards the rear of the ballroom. "I like you, Sadie Sinclair. It's a damned shame this is the first time I am meeting you."

"Likewise," Sadie agreed. After four years, three months, two weeks, three days, and approximately sixteen hours of being irrevocably, unrequitedly in love with Ella Beaufort, it was nice to be noticed, so she slid into the seat next to Clem right as the first course was being rolled out.

A waiter slid a bowl in front of her, the tendrils of steam curling up towards the ceiling as they left the chunks of potatoes and chives. She ate several demure spoonfuls, wishing she could be left alone to devour it. She'd barely eaten that day, nothing more than the muffin Ella had left on her desk that morning. Alas, the social mores of Verdance high society dictated she push the bowl away after less than half had been eaten. Her stomach ached in protest, human food never quite sating her, but she set the cutlery down on the tablecloth anyway.

Howard Evens continued to drone on, the keyboardist of the jazz combo beginning to slump over in her seat. "Shadows, he likes the sound of his own voice, doesn't he?" Clem whispered, covering her mouth with her hand. "He must think we all come here to listen to him talk about quarterly profits and witness preparation, and not to make nice with other attorneys and judges."

"Perhaps he'll be done soon," Sadie offered.

"I hope so, I have three people to meet with tonight." Clem traced a finger over Sadie's knuckle. "How about you, Ms. Sinclair?"

Sadie watched as Clem withdrew her hand, adjusting her bracelet. She was older, perhaps by ten years or so, but was easily the most stunning woman in the room. "I'm not meeting with anyone in particular," she replied. "I'm just here to show my face."

It was true in the sense that she didn't particularly enjoy the shallow small talk that accompanied galas; the half-truths and obfuscations reminded her too much of what had happened back home.

Howard Evens finally stopped talking, thank goodness, and as soon as the spotlight pivoted back to the band, Clem stood with her unfinished glass of champagne. "Keep my seat warm for me, Ms. Sinclair," she said. "I'll be back in two shakes."

Sadie nodded, adjusting the starched white napkin in her lap, hardly enough fabric to protect her dress in any practical sense. The scent of roasted meat wafted through the air, drawing saliva from beneath her tongue.

Char-grilled venison was pushed in front of her, alongside steamed asparagus and a thick rice dish with slices of large mushrooms adorning the top of the domed pile. Sadie picked at it, closing her eyes to reduce the temptation.

"Oh, thank the shadows, I'm half-starved," Clem said, depositing herself back into the seat and setting the pristine white cloth napkin in her lap. She sliced the meat into fifths, piling her fork with rice and vegetables too. "What's the matter, don't you eat?"

"Yes, I just..." Sadie trailed off. "No one really eats at these things, do they?"

Clem shoved the fork into her mouth, already loading up another bite. "My firm paid six hundred dollars for a table, I'm going to eat what I damned well please." She swallowed, taking a demure sip of her nearly empty champagne. "It's an awful waste otherwise, don't you think?"

"I never really thought of it that way," Sadie admitted, but followed suit, and her stomach was all the more grateful. A few couples finished their meals early, having left two-thirds on the plate, and moved onto the dance floor, swaying slowly beneath the twinkling lights of the dimmed grand chandelier. "Where did you go?" she asked. "Bidding at the silent auction?"

"Ms. Sinclair, we hardly know each other," Clem said with just the slightest hint of a southern drawl, likely brought on by the champagne. "I don't know if it's quite appropriate to be spilling all of our trade secrets, now is it?"

Sadie pushed her empty plate away, settling the fork and knife atop the porcelain. "I suppose not," she agreed. "Forgive my intrusion."

"I was speaking to the State's Attorney," Clem supplied, nodding to the other side of the ballroom. "He's here with his wife."

"I didn't think he came to these things."

"He doesn't." Clem drained her glass and set it on the table, running her finger around the rim. "Which is why I decided to do a little poking around. I think he may be running for Congress in the next election, he wants to get his face out there." She adjusted the silver fabric cut low across her chest, leaning into the table. "I imagine politics don't impact a small firm such as yours all that much?"

"You might be surprised," Sadie replied. "Things are different after the Rupture."

"Well, the Rupture changed everything, didn't it? All the monsters under the bed finally came out to play." Clem smoothed her hand over the white tablecloth, taking an errant wrinkle with her. "And with the monsters and the mythics, of course, came the politicians, and if there's anything a Verdance politician can't resist, it's money and power." She grimaced lightly, the frown surprisingly pretty on her face. "Rumor has it, he's in tight with that senator, Jonathan Dean."

Sadie stared out onto the dance floor, watching the darkened silhouettes as they spun and swayed, turning on parquet flooring, humoring the gala's organizers. "I try to stay out of the business of politics," she said finally. "Never seems to turn out well for anyone. Running for office is like putting a target on your back, don't you think?"

"Hmm," Clem uttered, pouring water from the carafe in the center of the table. "I can't say I disagree." She sipped at the water, condensed droplets forming a darkened ring under the glass. "Ms. Sinclair, do you want to get out of here?"

Sadie scanned the crowd, mentally dismissing every person she'd gone there to woo. "Yes," she said. "Why not?"

"Okay," Clem replied, and as she stood, whispered in Sadie's ear. "Your place or mine?"

#

Chapter Three

Clem's building was on the north side, with broad, sweeping fountains in the front, turned off for winter and crusted with old, frozen-over snow. The guard at the door stopped them, checking Clem's room key and staring at Sadie. "Guest?" he asked.

"Work meeting," Clem answered, breezing right past him. Reception was grand, with high ceilings and delicate lighting from the sconces on the walls, and an elevator as the centerpiece, glass and steel and a marvel of construction.

"Do you live here?" Sadie asked, appreciating the glitter of quartz inlaid into the marble tile foyer.

"No."

Sadie followed her onto the elevator, being sure to keep her hands away from the metal railings. "What firm are you with, again?" she asked, aware that the conversation had dried up in the cab on the ride over, despite Clem's questioning. "I missed it when you said earlier."

"I didn't say earlier," Clem replied casually, stepping off the elevator onto the seventh floor. "Tell me how you wound up in Verdance," she said. "It's pretty obvious you're not from around here."

Instinctively, Sadie reached for her hair, pulling it down over her ears. "Why do you say that?" she asked, cursing all the mirrors in that elevator, each one of them glaring her reflection back at her, ringed with the purple-pink hue of rifted guilt.

"Are you?" Clem pressed.

"No," Sadie admitted, but would never tell the full truth. She couldn't. "I grew up around the northern border," she answered. "I came to Verdance five or six years ago now."

Clem nodded, sliding her room key into the lock and disengaging it. The brass handle clicked as the latch released, and she pushed the heavy door open with her shoulder. "How are you finding it?"

"With a map," Sadie replied, attempting to shift the conversation back tomore comfortable ground. "Why, how do you find it?"

"Oh, I'm very well-traveled in these parts." Clem locked the door behind them both, and leaned against it, letting down her long blond hair until it trailed over her shoulders, halfway down her back. "I've found that I don't even need maps anymore."

Sadie let out a quiet hiss, playfully irritated that Clem had played her at her own game, something she was clearly skilled at doing. "I hope you will forgive a weary traveler for needing a map from time to time," she said softly. "After all, who could ever possibly know every path, every alleyway in Verdance? I find that I have a much more enjoyable experience if I ask for directions from time to time."

"Directions," Clem echoed, pushing herself off the door and catching Sadie by the wrists, holding her, but gently. "Yes, I suppose in some cases, that might be for the best. An unfamiliar commute, perhaps?"

"Or unfamiliar passengers," Sadie added, allowing herself to be cut off by Clem's kiss. Her lips were waxy with color, but she couldn't bring herself to care very much about the fact that she'd have it all over her body before too long.

"Where are you from?" Clem asked again, reaching for Sadie's zipper. "Which part of the northern border?"

Sadie resisted the urge to push away, enjoying the game far too much to be too concerned about the reason behind the ploy. "The northern part," she said, delighted to practice the art of obfuscation somewhere other than the interior of a courtroom. It had been a very long time since she'd danced with someone else the way she used to. "The very most northern part."

"I imagine the Verdance winters are nothing to you, then," Clem said, slowly releasing the dress from Sadie as the sleeves caught around her elbows. "And yet that overcoat you were wearing as we left seems to suggest otherwise."

"Better to be prepared," Sadie answered. "You only have to break down in a car once in this state to learn that lesson, and I learned it the first winter I was here." That much, at least, wasn't a lie. Sadie found the buttons of Clem's dress, releasing them one at a time. "I'm from a small place that no one here has ever heard of. In fact, they'd be surprised to discover it even exists."

Clem pressed her back onto the bed, the goose-down bedspread crunching under Sadie's weight. "And you came all the way here, to the big city," she continued. "To start a law practice?"

"Not much work for attorneys where I'm from." Sadie trailed a finger along the hem of Clem's dress, toying, teasing until she met flesh and dragged it up over Clem's thigh. "And as an industrious, hard-working patriot of this fine nation, I thought it was best to go where the work is."

"Mm, yes, you definitely strike me as the patriotic sort," Clem said with a husky laugh, pinning Sadie to the bed with a knee on either side. "That's why you're a private practice attorney, and not working for the feds."

Sadie pulled Clem closer, hands wrapped around her hips. "The federal building is a little too stifling for me. I prefer my surroundings to be a little more elegant."

"Like this dress?" Clem asked, sliding it down over Sadie's waist.

"Amongst other things."

Clem laid it carefully on the bed, leaving Sadie in her matching satin underthings. "It's classy," she complimented. "Understated. Something I was never quite able to achieve."

"You don't strike me as an understated woman." Sadie sat up, pulling the sleeves of Clem's dress down over her shoulders, running her hands over soft skin, reaching up to pull her down towards her mouth. "I would say quite the opposite." She planted a kiss against Clem's neck, drawing out a soft sigh. "How long have you been in contract law?"

"A few years," Clem replied, offering up her neck in sacrifice. "Before that, I was in family law."

"Family law," Sadie repeated, dragging her lips over the pulse point throbbing just beneath skin. She had the brief but insistent urge to bite, to feel Clem's artery between her too-sharp teeth, but bloodlust had never been a Fae purview. "I imagine that got very sticky after the Rupture."

"The stickiest," Clem agreed. "After about ten years of that, of mythics and mess, I decided that paperwork was much more my speed. Less chance you'll take a swipe from a shifter, you know what I mean?"

Sadie traced a fingertip across Clem's collarbones, lingering at the dip centered between them. "And have you taken many swipes?"

"I've managed to avoid any scarring, let's put it that way." Clem ran her hands up Sadie's form, coming to a rest at her waist, occasionally sliding back down to her hips. "Paperwork rarely bites back."

"Oh, I've seen paperwork take some nasty chunks out of people," Sadie argued, her tone light. Clem was looking for something, and Sadie was determined to not let her find it. "I've seen a folder ruin a life."

Clem laughed softly, pressing Sadie back into the bed again, laying kisses across her chest, running two fingertips along her legs. "Was it yours?"

"No," Sadie replied. "Opposing counsel's client."

"I guess you're the one taking bites out of everyone, then." Clem leaned down, her whispered breaths against Sadie's hidden ears drawing bumps from her skin. "A shame you didn't ask me first, I might have volunteered."

"Haven't you?" Sadie laughed, the sound ethereal and foreign even to herself. She trailed her fingers over the silk dress still resting at Clem's waist. Clem moved Sadie's hands to her neck, raising an eyebrow. Sadie leaned forward and dragged her teeth across Clem's throat, a gentle but dangerous pressure. Sadie pulled away again, staring at her in challenge. "Your move, Counselor."

"Is that a threat?"

"I guess that depends on what you're looking for." Sadie floated the words out, curious to see if Clem would take the bait, or let it drift by.

"Some fun after a very boring event," Clem answered, ignoring the tease. "I don't want to have gotten all gussied up for nothing."

"I think half of that ballroom was busy appreciating your presence," Sadie said. "It's one hell of a dress." She shifted her position on the bed, dropping her underthings to the floor. "I think I do prefer how it looks on the hanger, though. You're too much of an art exhibition to be covered up."

"Very sweet words from such a silver-tongued lawyer," Clem accused, ignoring the request. "I'm not sure if I believe you."

Sadie drew a knee up, resting her forearm on it. "Try me, then."

"Hmm," Clem murmured, returning to the bed but kneeling on the floor, dragging Sadie to the edge and gently biting where her femoral artery beat her half-human blood against the capillaries in her skin. Clem bit again, drawing a breathy flutter from Sadie's lungs that she hadn't realized was there.

"Still hungry?" she asked.

"I didn't get dessert," Clem replied, inching terribly closer until she was on Sadie, face buried where her thighs met.

As much as she wanted to, Sadie couldn't focus, her thoughts drifting back to Ella, the way they always did. She put on a good show, just the right amount of quiet cries, disguised as greediness, as wanting, but at the heart of them was a pervasive and inescapable longing that had long left a crater where something else should have been.

Clem sat on the bed, using the white handkerchief from her clutch to wipe the slick residue from her face. She reapplied her lipstick and blotted it before she did anything else, and then draped herself across the bed, laying an arm over Sadie's side.

"What agency do you work for?" Sadie asked, disentangling herself in order to reassemble her underthings. She was already dreading putting that dress back on, knowing she'd be frozen all the way home, even if she managed to find a cab heading east that time of night.

"I'm sorry?" Clem asked, all innocence and virtue, concealing whatever she was hiding beneath. "Which agency?"

"You're a private investigator," Sadie replied. "Either that, or you're working for the VCPD, which I doubt, or the feds, which I also doubt given you'd have no reason to need information from me." She flashed a grin at Clem over her shoulder.

Clem gave a quiet harrumph, sticking out her lower lip. "How long have you known?"

"Since the cab over here. You were entirely too interested in my back story for a one-night stand."

"Who said this was a one-night stand?"

Sadie pointed at her hand. "The fact that you're not wearing your wedding ring. I can see the line where it would usually be."

"Maybe I'm getting divorced."

"Does your husband know that this is how you glean information from unwilling marks?" Sadie asked evenly. She hadn't expected Clem to fold so easily, and couldn't help but wonder why. "Does he know where you are right now?"

Clem tilted her head, appraising Sadie. "I think that's none of your business."

"For the record," Sadie said, zipping up her dress, "I do come from the northern border. It is cold there, but there's something about Verdance that makes the chill harder to recover from. Even now, I'm betting you're craving that fluffy robe hanging on the back of the door. Go ahead, put it on. I'll wait."

"You must really think you're something else," Clem said, but stayed on the bed, her dress still half-zipped. "You never said where on the northern border."

"I said you'd never heard of it, and that much is true." Sadie glanced at her reflection in the wide mirror across from the bed, tugging her hair further down over her ears. She hated elaborate hairdos for that reason alone. "I can guarantee you that you've never heard of where I'm from, and I can also guarantee that I am from the northern border. I would swear on it, stake my own life on it, vow a solemn oath on my mother's grave to the truth of it."

Clem watched her from the bed, no doubt trying to discern the veracity of Sadie's claims. She wouldn't find anything, certainly not if seduction was her main form of finding a source. The Fae would see Clem coming from a mile off. They'd play with her and then discard her, the way they always did with their human toys.

"And because I know you'll be on the horn to the bar association the moment I leave this room, I should tell you that you won't find any law records prior to my arriving in Verdance," Sadie added after a moment.

"Because you've had them sealed? Or you changed your name to cover your tracks," Clem said, drawing circles in the fluffy bedspread with the tip of her finger.

"No," Sadie replied. "Nothing is sealed, and so long as I have been on this earth, my name has been Sadie Sinclair. I don't have a middle name. My mother thought that mine was quite enough as it is." She slipped her feet into her shoes, repressing the pained flinch when unyielding leather bit into her heels once more. "You can dig into my past forever, Clementine, you're not going to find anything."

\#

\#

Chapter Four

Morning in Verdance was a chaotic affair. As soon as the church bells rang out the seven-o'clock alarm, the streets were packed with automobiles, and the sidewalks were cluttered with people rushing to their jobs, rushing to school, rushing to get through the hours just to wind up one day closer to their inevitable demise. Mortality was something that still didn't make sense to Sadie. Time moved so much faster in the human realm, so much so that she'd already spotted fine lines at the corners of her eyes, despite her youth.

Sadie pushed into her office, kicking the slush from her boots. Spring was still weeks away, and a Verdance winter always did its best to cling on as long as possible.

"Good morning," Ella chirped from her desk, glancing up from the tall stack of paperwork in front of her. ' Long night?"

"Pardon?" Sadie asked, hanging her coat on the hook. The last thing the morning needed was reminders of the previous evening, and how it had ended.

"The gala," Ella prompted. "Was it nice?"

"Oh," Sadie replied. "Yes, it was similar to last year's event. I can't say there was much new to report. Although, Judge Liesse seemed to be suggesting I join a larger firm."

Ella leaned back in her chair and crossed one leg over the other, the soft charcoal grey wool of her skirt draped neatly over her knee. "And would you?" she asked. "Would you join someone else's firm?"

"What, and give up the best secretary this city has ever seen?" Sadie said, leafing through that morning's mail. "No. I've always been more of a loner."

"Muffin," Ella announced, pushing a slightly rumpled brown paper bag across her desk. "I got you the blueberry."

"My favorite." Sadie collected the bag and along with it, a steaming mug of black coffee, fresh from the percolator. "What would I do without you?"

Ella shrugged. "Starve."

"How was your anniversary date?" Sadie asked, determined to be polite even if the thought of Ella with Ray turned her stomach more than any of the crime scene photos she'd been privy to. "Nice, I hope?"

"Sure, The Saffron Rose is always nice. Good food, luxurious ambiance."

"But?"

"The couple at the next table got engaged!" Ella exclaimed, burying her face in her hands. "It was beautiful, she cried, the ring was absolutely gorgeous, Sadie, honestly you should have seen it. I congratulated them, and Ray spent the rest of the night in some kind of awful mood." Ella groaned, the sound muffled by her fingers. "He probably thought I'd be angling for a proposal last night, but I wasn't!"

"No?" Sadie knew better than to allow that pin-prick of hope to penetrate the callused exterior of her heart, but she asked anyway.

Ella shook her head. "No!" She raised her head off the desk, looking apologetic. "I wanted to talk to you about something."

"Oh?" Sadie was struggling to temper her thoughts, averting her eyes. "Tell me."

"This is hard for me to say," Ella whispered, emotion thick in her voice. "You know me, Sadie, I'm afraid of rejection and I would never want to jeopardize our friendship. Working here for you has been the best three years of my life, and while I've been thinking about this for six months already, I just couldn't bring myself to say it out loud because I've been worried that you wouldn't—" she faltered, staring up at Sadie with helpless eyes, round and deep brown with desperation ringed around her irises.

"Wouldn't what?" Sadie pressed, her heart thudding in her chest.

"Keep me on here," Ella finished. She stood up, smoothing the wrinkles from her skirt and matching jacket with nervous hands, fidgeting with the hem. "I want to be a paralegal."

Never before had Sadie come crashing back to earth with such incredible speed, and the impact was astounding. "A paralegal," she repeated.

"I know that there isn't much budget for a raise right now, but the courses will take me at least six months of night school to complete, plus I'll have to pass my exams, so it wouldn't be for a while yet," Ella explained. "I know that's not why you hired me, so I will understand if—"

"I think that's a great idea," Sadie interjected. "I've always wanted a paralegal."

"You—you have?" Ella asked. "Then why didn't you get one?"

Sadie shrugged easily, despite the storm of competing emotions swirling within her. "I suppose the right one never came along. Until now."

"Oh," Ella said softly, breathing out a relieved sigh. "I'm so glad! I love working here, and I'd love to keep doing that as long as I can."

"Which school?" Sadie asked, edging into her office so that she could at least hide whatever was happening on her face. She checked the mirror hanging on the back of the file cabinet and winced at the flushed, pink-cheeked reflection that stared back at her. "And who is the teacher?"

Ella chewed her lip before she answered. "Division College. Judge Liesse is the instructor for my introduction to law course. It started last week."

"That explains the questions, she knows that you're my recep—that you're working here," Sadie corrected herself. "Why did you think I'd be upset?"

"I don't know, I suppose I thought you'd want things to stay as they are."

"You will be a fantastic paralegal," Sadie replied evenly. "You already are in a lot of ways, Ella. You were born for the law." She set the muffin and the coffee on her desk, turning so the handle faced due south. It was the only part of her she would allow to have a modicum of nostalgia for home. "You could be a lawyer if you wanted. You have the smarts and the tenacity."

"I don't know if that would be... appropriate," Ella said from the doorway, perfectly positioned between the frame with her hands clasped in front of her. "Ray supports me working, but I imagine I'd have to give it up if—when we had children."

Sadie made some sort of indiscernible sound in her throat, something between acknowledgment and revulsion. Ray was a good-looking, handsome man, and he knew it. He'd use his influence to keep her at a manageable level, and not allow Ella to spread her wings like she deserved to. "Did you say there was a meeting this morning?"

On cue, Astrid Frost jangled through the front door, her fur coat dusted with powdery snow and the seven necklaces around her throat clinking against each other noisily.

"Good morning, Ms. Frost," Ella chimed, pulling her folder from the cabinet. "It's lovely to see you again."

"Sadie, we have a problem," Astrid announced, ignoring Ella entirely to flounce into Sadie's office, depositing herself in the padded armchair across the desk and shrugging off her coat. She turned and took the file from Ella, closing the door in her face from her seated position. "I think I have an informant in my club."

"Good morning," Sadie echoed, taking the file and spreading the pages out on her desk. "How can I assist you?"

"Someone fed the VCPD information about my business, and now I'm spending all my time looking over my shoulder." Astrid huffed angrily, pointing at the papers smudged with newsprint ink. "If I don't find out who it is, I'm going to wind up in prison." She leaned across the desk, her palms pressed into the laminated wood. "And I can't go to prison."

Sadie reached for a pen and a notepad simultaneously, ready to get to work for her worst and most demanding client. Astrid was unfortunately also her richest client. "That may be putting the cart before the horse, Ms. Frost," she demurred. "Has law enforcement visited your premises?"

"Not this week, no, but lately," Astrid explained. "All that mess with…" she glanced around at the door, making sure that it was closed. "With Frankie Fiske."

"You told me you didn't have business with him when we discussed how he went missing," Sadie said.

"Not *directly*."

"Ah." Sadie flipped down the notepad's cover, setting the pen aside. "I'd recommend a private investigator at this stage, and as you already have one available to you five, I—"

"No, no, I can't use Vee," Astrid said, waving a hand in protest. "A few of my bouncers caught on to her sniffing around the club. They won't say anything to her. Besides, she still acts like a cop."

"I was under the impression that Virginia Vane was the top private investigator in the city," Sadie replied. "Surely if she's been around the club, she may have noticed something interesting, or overheard some commentary."

Astrid shook her head. "She's not an option. Trust me on that."

"Did you have a disagreement?"

"Let's just say we're not on good terms."

"Okay," Sadie said, knowing not to pry when it came to Astrid. "Then I suggest we find another private investigator. One who looks and sounds authentic, and won't raise any eyebrows." She took a sip of the coffee, flinching at the unwelcome acrid taste. She enjoyed the caffeine but hated the taste. The muffin, however, was much more palatable, and she took several bites as Astrid looked on with disdain.

"That's asking for a lot in Verdance," Astrid argued. "Too many people know, or at least suspect what I am." She crossed her legs at the knees, bouncing her foot with such exuberance that the heel of her shoe was sliding to the floor. "I don't want to wind up on the wrong side of this, Sadie. I don't want to end up in prison."

"That's what I'm here for," Sadie said, trying to reassure her. "To keep you out of jail."

"Someone is gunning for me," Astrid insisted. "I need to know who, and I need to know why." She hid her mouth behind her hand, as if there was anyone else in the room who would hear her. "My bartender wound up dead in my basement with his eyes pulled out," she whispered.

"When did this happen?" Sadie asked, swallowing back the gasp that pulled at her throat. "Do you know who did it?"

"No, but I can only assume it was a crew job," Astrid answered. "No one else would have done things like that."

Sadie nodded, keeping her eyes fixed on the papers in front of her. "To what end?"

"I don't know, maybe it was one crew trying to send a message to the other about turf. I know that Bryce got supplies from the Ruby Thorns, but I wasn't involved in the procuring of anything."

Sadie nodded. "Good," she said, and added, "I'm sorry to hear about your bartender.

"Thank you," Astrid replied, barbed, but there was a flicker of a flinch in the way she moved her wrist. "I don't want to wind up at the bottom of a ravine thanks to some crew, and I also don't want to see the inside of a cell. Are we clear?"

Sadie leaned back, closing the folder and straightening the edges of the pages inside. "Crystal, Ms. Frost." She chose her next words carefully, aware that one wrong move would take twenty five percent of her yearly earnings if Astrid Frost walked out of her office. "Is there any possibility that Virginia Vane was the police informant?"

"No."

"How can you be sure?"

Astrid hummed angrily, the notes barbed with betrayal. "I'm sure. If it was her, I'd be in prison already. She's all cozied up with Captain Lindell, or whatever her name is. Tall, broad. A voice like salted honey but the demeanor of a werewolf at a solstice." She adjusted the sparkling bracelet at her wrist, positioning it perfectly against her bone, dark skin gleaming in the reflections of the diamonds. "It's not Vee. It's someone else."

"Last I heard, she was working with the VCPD on the Fiske stuff. I'd heard that she got caught in a significant physical altercation," Sadie said casually, knowing full well that Astrid had a much more sordid and personal history with Virginia Vane than she liked to admit.

"I hadn't heard that," Astrid said after a moment, shifting uncomfortably in her seat. "What happened?"

"I don't know the details." Sadie tucked the folder into her desk drawer, along with the unused notepad, closing it with a sharp snap. "You would have to ask Ms. Vane the details of what occured."

"She's out of town, I already tried."

"Either way, you will need another private investigator. What's the fee?" Sadie asked, leaning back in her chair, and crossing her legs. Astrid scowled, but didn't say anything about it.

"Enough."

"And what is the cover story?" Sadie pressed.

Astrid shifted in her seat, tugging her fur coat back up over her bare shoulders. "New bartender, to replace Bryce. I already have someone in mind, but it can't be me who reaches out on an official number. Can you do that?"

"I will add it to your invoice."

"Of course, everything with you is billable," Astrid shot back, acid dripping from every syllable. "Her name is Clementine Dorefield."

Blood turned to ice in Sadie's veins, freezing her in place. "Clementine?" she asked, praying to gods she'd never even believed in that she'd heard wrong. "Clem?"

"Oh, you've met!" Astrid exclaimed, a smile spreading across her perfectly portioned face, all the way up to her high cheekbones, tinted with blush. "Fabulous, then I imagine this won't be a problem at all."

Sadie swallowed hard, willing her lungs to resume their usual function. "Do you have a number for her?"

"No. Don't you?"

Astrid stared long enough to unsettle Sadie again, and so she cleared her throat in apology. "I'll track one down, Ms. Frost."

"See that you do. This is of utmost urgency. For all I know, someone is already feeding the VCPD incriminating—and may I be candid, *false*—information about how I choose to run my business. It's no one's business but mine what I choose to sell, and I'm not doing anything other than what every other club in this damned city is doing." Astrid stood, tugging her coat around her until it was cinched at her perfect waist. "I'm being targeted, Ms. Sinclair. This is because I'm a mythic."

"It's certainly possible," Sadie agreed. "We shouldn't rule anything out."

"It's that Captain Lindell. She has it out for me because I'm a siren. There aren't even that many of us left, and she'd have me thrown in jail just because some of my bouncers and bartenders like to make a few extra dollars on the side shifting Nether." She laid her hand on the doorknob, her fingernails polished a light pink. "I shouldn't be held responsible for what others do, just because it happens to be my name on the lease."

"Understood, Ms. Frost." Sadie stood to shake her hand, but Astrid didn't extend hers. "I'll track down this investigator and get back to you."

Chapter Five

Astrid hadn't been gone two hours before the front door creaked open again, and Ella's cautious tone dragged at Sadie's ear.

"Can I help you?" Ella asked from her desk, standing to match the man who had just entered.

"Are you Sadie Sinclair, esquire?" the man asked, staring down at the envelope.

"I'm her receptionist. I can take that for you." Ella reached for it, but he yanked it out of her grasp, holding it over his head. "Sorry, ma'am, it has to go to Ms. Sinclair directly."

Sadie leaned against the door frame of her office, examining her cuticles casually. "Who is it from?"

"Who?" the man repeated, still holding the letter aloft.

"It's a note from Ms. Frost, yes?" Sadie said, nodding towards it. "You're one of her employees. You're a bouncer at the Sphinx, if I remember correctly."

He shifted his weight from foot to foot, edging backward towards the door. "She told me to be sure it was for your eyes only."

Sadie laughed easily, despite the knot forming in her stomach, probably getting an early start on an ulcer. "This is a law office, not a club. Everyone employed here has Ms. Frost's best interests at heart." She held her hand out, gesturing for him to hand it over. "The letter, please."

"I, uh..." he trailed off, laying the envelope in Sadie's outstretched palm. "Thank you. I mean, you're welcome."

When he'd left, and the door closed, Sadie tore through the envelope's seal, leaving an ugly, ragged scar across the top of it. She stared at the blocky black and white print, hissing a sigh out through gritted teeth.

"What did she say?" Ella prompted, still standing behind her desk. "What happened?"

"Ms. Frost has received a subpoena," Sadie said. "Looks like she was right, someone is after her. She's probably being tailed too, if I had to guess." She cast a suspicious glance at the phone on Ella's desk and flipped the receiver off the hook, letting it fall to the desk. "Don't use the phones. If she's being subpoenaed, our lines might be tapped, too."

"At all?" Ella asked. "But how will clients get hold of us?"

Sadie replaced the receiver into the cradle with a frown, wishing for the forty-seventh time that month that she'd chosen some other profession to land in the human realm with. The law was fascinating, but at times, supremely irritating. "Be mindful of what you say over the phone. Appointments only, no messages."

"Of course," Ella agreed. "When does she have to go in?"

"No date yet, but soon." She glanced at the letter again and frowned, tempted to tear up the letter as if that would undo the legality of the subpoena. "I have a feeling that this is Ed Link again. I swear, that man is just angry I keep beating him in court." She tossed it onto her desk, where it slid across the smooth surface before coming to a rest right at the edge, teetering at the beveled wood. "As if I didn't have ten million other things I'd rather be doing."

"Feel free to delegate," Ella offered, adjusting a pin at the back of her head, securing the tail of her coiled braid. "Did you want me to go looking for this investigator for Astrid?"

Sadie looked at her from the corner of her eye. "You heard that?"

"These doors aren't very thick."

"Good to know." Sadie drummed her fingertips against her desk, briefly wondering if it was worth using what was left of her Fae magic to get free of whatever trap the VCPD was setting with Ed's help. "This isn't just about Astrid. It's about me, too."

"Prosecutors rarely like defense attorneys," Ella said. "I don't think it matters that it was you, he'd have sent a subpoena regardless."

"I don't know why they bother with this, Astrid's finances are pristine." Sadie continued to tap a rhythm into the wood with her hands, closing her eyes to go over the details she knew to be true. "Was Virginia Vane subpoenaed?" she asked aloud, before shaking her head. "No, Astrid said she was out of town, they won't have been able to serve her. Ella, see if you can track her down. She's a client, we should have her address on file. I doubt she's moved, she's a creature of habit."

Ella nodded, sitting to jot notes down. "Don't worry," she said as she wrote. "I'll take notes in code. We don't want anything that could be intercepted."

"What would I do without you?" Sadie asked, for the second time that day. "Be disbarred and starve, probably," she answered herself. "Thank you."

"Just doing my job, Sadie," Ella replied with an apologetic smile. "What are the odds they have something solid on Astrid?"

Sadie drew invisible patterns into the wood as she considered the implications of the subpoena and specifically, Edward Link. "They'll know that the Sphinx is financially and ethically sound," she posited under her breath. "So why bring her in? What do they expect to find?"

Realization dropped into her like a brick. "Ella, get me everything on that new federal law that was proposed. The one about national security."

"What does Astrid have to do with the military, or with anything federal?" Ella asked, already dragging out a thick binder stuffed full with bar association notices about proposed changes to federal and state law, pages spilling out over the sides and fluttering to the ground.

"Everything, if they know for sure she is a mythic selling Nether," Sadie said. "If this Lindell is after her, she'll use anything and everything she can to make an example of her, including drug distribution and public endangerment." She raised an appreciative eyebrow, despite the situation. "Clever. Irritating, but clever. That law hasn't passed yet, but they expect it to soon."

"Are you going to tell Astrid about this law?" Ella asked, the warm glow of the incandescent light bulbs in their fixtures playing off the gold flecks in her eyes.

"No, she'll just panic, and this might be nothing more than a fishing expedition." Sadie scowled at the letter, still hesitating as it teetered at the edge of the desk. "If we're lucky, that's all it is, meant to keep Astrid quiet and pliable whilst they track down something else." She unbuttoned and rebuttoned the links at her cuffs. "It could be worse. If that law had already passed, it could have been a subpoena for me."

"For you?" Ella tilted her head, eyes squinted in confusion. "Why?"

Sadie dragged out a relatively new slice of newspaper, the print still crisp. "This new law I mentioned, the one proposed by Jonathan Dean, you know, J.D., one of our senators?" She flexed her jaw, a silent, almost invisible display of irritation. "He has posited that the Nether trade should be considered beneath the banner of terrorism. That would give them the right to subpoena Ms. Frost's legal representation."

"But that's illegal," Ella protested. "Attorney-client privilege—"

"Would be stripped," Sadie finished. "A huge breach of ethics, of course, and of constitutional rights, but it seems that Senator Dean doesn't hold either in very high regard, with the exception of Human Rights, of course." She hissed out a Fae curse under her breath before she could catch herself, trying to cover the elided syllables with a coarse clear of her throat.

Ella slid the paper back across the table. "At least it hasn't passed yet," she offered, but all Sadie could hear was the heavy weight of the word *yet* tacked to the end of the reassurance.

"We should prepare for that possibility," Sadie said, tucking it back into the binder, accidentally fraying one of the edges as it snagged on the metal ring. "I fear it may be more of an inevitability, the way things are going."

The door to the place next door, a bakery, opened and closed with a squeak and the loud jingle of the bells attached. The morning's muffin felt too far away, Sadie craved distraction from the news of the subpoena. "Lunch?" she asked.

"Always," Ella answered, already grabbing her bag from under the desk and preparing to lock the office door. "Are you going to tell Astrid about the tap?"

"I don't know if there is one yet. It's best to wait. Let's see if Ed Link is in bed with the feds, they're probably tailing me." Sadie stepped out into the chilly afternoon and reached back inside for her coat. Even next door was too far to travel without it. Parked on the street, there was a smattering of vehicles, some she recognized as belonging to another shop's occupants along the road, and others she didn't. Her eyes fell on a brand new black model V, designed by one of Verdance's foremost residents, some rich fool named Dwayne Williamson who made his money stealing everyone else's inventions.

Two men sat inside, both in black wool coats and sharp hats pulled down to obscure their faces. They were feds, they had to be.

"Watch your step," Sadie warned in Ella's direction, nodding almost imperceptibly at the car. "It looks like I was right after all."

"Good to know, at least," Ella said. She strode past Sadie towards the street with a feminine smile, her t-strap heels clicking confidently against the concrete.

"Ella!" Sadie hissed, but her insistent whisper didn't stop her. "What are you doing?"

Her skirt swung behind her, the hem dancing at Ella's calf. She swayed with every step as she neared the car. "Good afternoon, gentlemen!" she chirped, waving at their driver's side window. "I noticed you've been out here for a while, did you need help? Directions? If you're worried about coming into the law practice, it's absolutely fine, totally normal," she said. Her voice drifted along the yellowed grass, the snow atop it clinging on until spring had finally sprung.

The man in the driver's seat mumbled something and quickly pulled away from the curb, jerking the car into the traffic of the lunch rush.

"What did he say?" Sadie asked as Ella approached. "Why did they leave?"

"He said they were looking at a map," Ella replied. "And he was sorry for taking up a parking space for so long." She tapped one shoe and then another against the sidewalk, dislodging the errant snow that had collected against the heels. "Definitely feds, though. You know the type."

"How do you know so much?"

Ella shrugged. "Learned from the best." She pulled open the bakery's door, letting loose the warm, thick scent of freshly baked bread. "The usual?"

"Yes please," Sadie agreed, unsettled by the morning's events but doing her best to remain stoic. "May I have extra cheese on mine?"

Pointing through the glass counter display, Ella ordered for the both of them. "Two specials," she announced. "Extra cheese on both, if you don't mind. Practicing law is a hungry business."

The surly baker nodded, the way he always did. He took two fat slabs of spongy bread, slathering them with a herbed tomato sauce, peppers, and a tower of cheese, sliding them into a large, brick oven. Ella slid the money across the counter and joined Sadie in the lone booth, a tear gracing the upper right quarter of the seat back. White stuffing peeked out at the sides, but with food that good and that cheap, Sadie knew better than to pay it too much attention.

"You shouldn't have done that, you know," she murmured under her breath. "Spoken to those feds, I mean. For all we know, that just put you on their radar."

"It let them know that we're watching," Ella challenged. "That we are vigilant, and they can't sneak up on us. We're smarter than they think."

Sadie drummed two fingers against the cheap, chipped countertop. "I suppose that's true," she relented. "But I don't like the idea of you getting into trouble."

"What's life without a little danger?" Ella asked coyly, sliding a plate over to Sadie when the baker deposited them. "I doubt they'll come back."

"I don't, they'll just be quieter next time." Sadie took a bite of the steaming rectangle, grateful for its savory distraction. "We'll have to start making note of which cars are parked out front and when. We don't want any other clients getting embroiled in this by accident." Cheese elongated as she took another bite, a long, thin strand of melted beauty extending from her mouth to the baked dough until she deposited it into her mouth. Her father probably would have fainted at the sight of so much fried dough. He'd always loved human delicacies. "As much as I dislike Ms. Frost, she brings us too much business. We need to ascertain who this informant is, and fast." Sadie set her food down, unfolding her napkin into her lap. "We're going to have to call

Clementine Dorefield."

"I'll do it after lunch," Ella offered, cutting her food into small, polite bites. "We might have to pay a priority fee."

"No!" Sadie replied, a little too noisily, drawing the ire of the baker. She cleared her throat lightly and picked up the dough again. "No," she repeated. "I'll call."

#

#

Chapter Six

Sadie had always disliked the feds. Aggressive and cocky, with egos inflated beyond the size of most blimps. Most federal prosecutors thought themselves beyond godliness, and it showed in their every action, from the shine of their boring shoes to how much pomade they had in their hair.

She adjusted her double-breasted blazer, sharply cut with a navy-colored wool shot through with tiny tweed flecks. It was the nicest suit she owned, and the price tag proved it. If she was going to beat the preliminary hearing, she'd have to look the part of a suave, confident, *human* defense attorney, not an excommunicated half-Fae who'd lost the most important court battle of her queendom's existence.

"All rise," the bailiff droned, standing next to the judge's bench. "Honorable Judge Liesse presiding."

Sadie's shoulders tensed with reflective frustration. The judge's comments at the gala had nothing to do with Ella. She was trying to warn Sadie about the potential of a grand jury indictment. A larger firm would have granted her more protections, just by way of red tape and paperwork.

The judge gestured for them all to sit and she laid the gavel on the bench, staring down the prosecution. "I'm to understand we are here today with a subpoena for the ongoing Nether trade case. Mr. Prosecutor, you intend to progress to a grand jury indictment for Ms. Frost on the charges of drug distribution?"

"Mr. Novak," the prosecutor asserted. "Pleased to be here, ma'am, thank you for seeing us in your court at such short notice." He shuffled some papers around, bringing a clipboard to the forefront. "Today we will be hearing testimony from Mr. Gibson, an eyewitness to the sale and distribution of Nether in Ms. Frost's club, The Sphinx."

Sadie had always found it strange, asking witnesses to swear allegiance to a book. Religion wasn't relevant in the Fae realm, at least, not unless you counted the idolatry of the court.

"I swear," Mr. Gibson replied to the bailiff, pressing his hand against a book covered with old, cracked, black leather. He held a green wool flat cap in his hands, twisting it one way, and then the next. It wasn't anxiety that forced his movements, it was a quiet, pulsing anger that throbbed just beneath his skin, radiating out through his eyes as he glared at Astrid sitting behind the defense desk.

Novak prowled across the courtroom, putting on a show despite the absence of a jury. "Mr. Gibson," he began, glancing at the note cards he had stacked in his palm. "When did you last see your wife?"

"Objection," Sadie interrupted, standing. "Relevance, Your Honor."

"I've barely gotten started, Ms. Sinclair, and already you're bent on undermining this poor man's testimony," Novak replied casually. "Your Honor, I assure you, the relevance will become crystal clear."

Judge Liesse frowned. "Overruled. Mr. Novak, keep it tight, if you please, some of us have a full docket today."

"Of course." Novak shuffled through his note cards, straightening his shoulders and standing to his full, imposing height. "Mr. Gibson, if you please sir, when was the last time you saw your wife?"

"Two months ago."

"And when was the last time your two daughters saw their mother?"

Sadie stood again. "Objection," she stated. "I fear Mr. Novak's strategy is one that has very little bearing on Ms. Frost's innocence or otherwise."

"Overruled," the judge said again. "Let's give him a chance, shall we, Ms. Sinclair?"

"Yes, Your Honor," Sadie replied, sitting back down. She straightened the hem of her jacket, trying not to give away her quiet irritation at Novak's line of questioning.

Mr. Gibson cleared his throat. "My daughters haven't seen their mother for two months, either, I'm afraid."

"And why is that?" Novak asked, ready to read from the next note card.

"My wife is a Nether addict," the man replied, emotion snagging the edges of his tone. He pulled and twisted at the hat in his lap, popping one of the stitches at the brim with the quiet snap of wool thread. "Has been for about a year now."

"Where did your wife obtain these illegal drugs?" Novak asked gently, responding admirably to the man's obvious distress.

"The Sphinx," Gibson replied, brow furrowed both with defiance and determination to get through the questioning without losing his composure. Sadie had seen the same thing dozens of times. He pointed at Astrid, sitting there in her demure black dress with a straight hem halfway down her calf, one knee crossed over the other as she bounced with frustrated anxiety. "Her club," he added. "It's where my wife got everything she ever took."

"Horseshit," Astrid muttered under her breath. "We don't serve addicts in my club."

"Shh," Sadie urged without looking at her. There were elements of Astrid's business that had never sat well with her, but in Verdance, and as the humans liked to say, sometimes it was safer with the devil you knew than the one you didn't.

"How do you know that's where your wife obtained these drugs?" Novak asked, approaching the stand with a relaxed, kindly stance he'd never show to a defendant.

"She told me," Gibson replied.

"Objection," Sadie said again, but this time, she heard the waver in her own voice, knowing it was entirely possible that the man was telling the truth. "Hearsay."

"And I saw her once," Gibson added, not even waiting for the judge's ruling.

"Overruled, as such," the judge said. "Please continue, Mr. Gibson."

He nodded. "I followed her one night—left my girls with my mother, of course—and I saw her go into the club. I went in, kept to the shadows. It's not hard in a place like that, especially on a Friday night." He swallowed hard, fingers digging into the stiff brim of the hat. "I watched my wife flip a few bills to a bartender, and in return she got two cocktails and two vials of that stuff."

Novak nodded, shuffling through the cards. "For the court please, sir, can you specify what you mean by *that stuff*?"

"Nether." Gibson practically growled the word, too many weeks of his wife's absence having made the heart grow calloused. "She disappeared into the ladies' room, came out with purple tinges around her eyes looking like a two-bit—" he stopped himself, shaking his head. "I apologize, Your Honor. I shouldn't use such language in a court of law."

"Thank you for your restraint, Mr. Gibson," Judge Liesse responded, waving a hand towards him. "You may continue."

"Two more vials that night, but she put those into her handbag for later," Gibson said. "I confronted her in the alley at closing, when the club dumped everyone out onto the streets. Said I knew what she'd been doing, where she'd been going. She denied it all, of course, even though she could barely stand up. I wouldn't take her home to our girls, not in that state. I put her in a cab to her mother's place on the west side."

"And where is your wife now?" Novak asked.

Gibson's mouth pressed into a thin line before he gathered the courage to answer. "I don't know."

Silence hung over the courtroom, the implications of his testimony as weighty as they were fraught. Even Astrid had stilled her nervous fidgeting at Sadie's side.

"She never made it to her mother's that night," Gibson continued. "Probably tipped the cab driver extra to take her somewhere else, I don't know. She hasn't come home, not for me, and not for our girls." He turned towards Astrid again, and this time, the anger percolating at his jugular had stilled like cold magma turned to permanence. "She was a good mother before she got into Nether, you know," he said. "Loved those girls like they were the last light in Verdance. I don't much care if she's fallen out of love with me, Ms. Frost, that can happen with men and women, but for her to fall out of love with her daughters, well, that's just unnatural." He leaned forward, pressing against the stand. "It's a sickness, a rot in this city, and the roots are in that club of yours."

"Do something," Astrid hissed out of the side of her mouth, pressing herself backwards into the hard wood back of the chair. "Can't you object to that?"

Sadie tried to pull herself up out of the chair, but struggled under the man's pained stare. "Er—objection, Your Honor," she said. "Speculation?"

The judge's eyes flicked from Mr. Gibson, to Astrid, and then to Sadie. "Yes, Ms. Sinclair. Sustained." Judge Liesse straighted the pages on the bar, stacking them neatly before sliding them back into their file. "Do you have more questions for your witness, Mr. Novak?" she asked.

"Just one, Your Honor." He tucked his note cards back into his breast pocket, disturbing the unmatched pocket square there. "Mr. Gibson, did you see any other patrons purchase Nether at the Sphinx that night from the bar?"

"I did," the man answered. "Several."

"No further questions."

Judge Liesse nodded, making a note on the paper in front of her. "Ms. Sinclair, you can cross-examine the prosecution's witness, if you wish."

"Yes, Your Honor," Sadie said, abandoning her notes on the desk. She'd anticipated a witness, of course, but she hadn't anticipated one quite so sympathetic that his story tugged at her own heartstrings, even after all she'd seen in Verdance. She approached the witness stand slowly, not yet quite sure what she was going to say. "Good morning, Mr. Gibson," she said. "Thank you for your service to the court."

"It's my duty as a citizen of this country," he replied gruffly. "Someone has to stand up against what's happening, what's been happening since the Rupture."

Sadie nodded. "Of course, sir," she said. "And I'm very sorry to hear about your wife."

He didn't say anything, glaring past her at Astrid once again before being brought back to attention by Novak's noisily cleared throat.

"Mr. Gibson," Sadie began, "what did this bartender look like?"

"Tall, dark hair, broad-shouldered. Wore their standard uniform of a black shirt, but his sleeves were rolled up to the elbows."

"And when did you witness this sale of Nether?" Sadie asked.

"Just before my wife went missing, so around two months ago," he replied.

Sadie breathed out a restrained breath, feeling the pressure of Astrid's eyes boring into her back as she worked. She returned to her desk, tugging a photograph from the file. "Mr. Gibson, was this the bartender your wife purchased Nether from?"

He leaned forward, considering the picture. "Looks like him, yes,"

"Your Honor, the bartender in question is Bryce Callwell, who is now, unfortunately, deceased." Sadie handed it to the judge before turning back to the witness. "Given Bryce Callwell's mysterious and unforseen demise, Mr. Gibson, do you think it's possible that he was the only one profiting from the sale of Nether in Ms. Frost's club? After all, she—"

"Objection," Novak interrupted. "Beyond the scope. Mr. Gibson is not a detective, nor is he an investigator."

"Sustained," the judge agreed. "Be careful, Ms. Sinclair."

Sadie clenched her jaw behind a tight-lipped smile. "Yes, Your Honor, of course." She glanced back at Astrid, whose usually confident demeanor was quickly melting into the shining marble tiles of the courtroom floor. "Mr. Gibson, did you see Ms. Frost exchange Nether for money at any point that evening?"

"No."

"And did you see her use Nether, or have any on her person?"

Gibson popped another stitch from the hat. "*No.*"

"No further questions," Sadie relented. "Thank you for your time, sir."

Novak, poised to pounce, did just that. "Your Honor, we have further witnesses to present to the court who have not yet responded to their subpoena. It's believed they may be out of town."

"I imagine you'd like a continuance, Mr. Novak?" Judge Liesse asked, pen ready in her hand. "I can offer you a week to get this witness into court."

"We'll make it happen, Your Honor."

"Good. Dismissed." The judge smacked the gavel lightly against the bench and disappeared back into her chambers, black robes flowing dramatically after her.

"What was that?" Astrid demanded, knee bouncing once more. "You could have asked him far more than you did, Ms. Sinclair, and you're just letting them skate by."

"He's a sympathetic witness, Ms. Frost," Sadie explained, watching Mr. Gibson advance on the desk out of the corner of her eye. "Going too hard on him would only hurt you more than that very damaging testimony already did." She closed the folder and tucked it into her briefcase, snapping it closed. "There's only so much we can do to pin this on the deceased. As a club owner, you still have obligations and responsibilities where illegal substances are concerned."

Mr. Gibson stopped at the desk, staring down at Astrid. "I don't think you understand what that stuff does to people," he said quietly.

"Sir, it's best if you refrain from speaking to my client," Sadie interrupted, far more concerned with what Astrid could say than what he would.

"This is—was—my wife," he said, setting a small, wallet-sized photo on the desk. A pretty woman with light eyes and a string of long pearls stared back at them with a broad, gleaming smile that reached all the way across her face. "This is whose life you've ruined, hers and my daughters'," he said. Backing away from the table, he held his hands up. "That's all."

Astrid examined the picture, unfamiliar lines deepening across her forehead with every short moment that passed. She handed it to a man sitting just behind her in the gallery. "Make sure this gets put behind the bar. If she comes in, don't serve her a damned thing. And make a note of it somewhere."

"Aye, ma'am," the bouncer replied, concealing it in his inside breast pocket. "We'll make sure it's done."

Sadie watched as two little girls waited outside the court, both the spitting image of their mother, tended to by a woman she could only assume was Mr. Gibson's mother. The girls both hugged their father, one taking each leg and holding on with such a fierce desperation that it pulled at some thread in Sadie so hard it threatened to snap.

"The club will never survive if it gets a reputation as a hovel for Nether-heads," Astrid said with her usual haughtiness, but Sadie couldn't help but notice a strange hollowness beneath the words that hadn't been there before.

#

#

#

Chapter Seven

Despite not seeing the car that had been sitting outside the office, Sadie took three buses and a cab, doubling back on herself twice to lose anyone who might be following her. It was dark already, the spring solstice still over a month away, and the evenings cold with a kind of bone-chilling tremor that sank deep beneath the skin. The Verdance winters were so much longer than where she'd grown up on the northern border of Nos Prehn, and the icicles hanging from the back door awning of the Sphinx would be omnipresent for at least a few more weeks.

Sadie pushed past the bouncer, thrusting a business card into his hand. "I have a meeting with Ms. Frost," she said, already making her way down the long corridor.

"You can't go up there," he protested, trailing after her.

"I can promise you that is not the case," she retorted. Going to the Sphinx was among her most hated chores. The entire place stank of gin, the interior was tacky and overblown, and the keening, wailing women in the ladies' restroom during Astrid's performances were too much to handle, sober or not. "We need to talk," she announced at the doorway to Astrid's dressing room, the overly warm temperature already drawing sweat from her underarms.

"What are you doing here?" Astrid asked coldly, powdering her nose with quick, sharp movements. "You should have called."

"Your phones are probably tapped," Sadie said evenly, expecting an eruption, and bracing for it.

Astrid threw down the soft, talc-laden puff in her hand, and it landed on the counter in a cloud of pink particles. "What?" she snapped, whirling around in her chair. "Why are they tapping my phones?"

"Hoping to catch you talking to your suppliers, I would imagine. Make sure you're doing everything in person."

Astrid rolled her huge brown eyes dramatically. "Suppliers, and which of my suppliers exactly?" she said coyly. "Ever since Fiske disappeared—"

"I would recommend that you resist the impulse to be cavalier in your words, Ms. Frost," Sadie cautioned. "We don't know who may or may not be listening."

"There's nothing out there," Astrid continued. "No one can lay their hands on *catering supplies*, not me, no one. '

"Regardless, you'll need to keep that in mind whenever you or anyone else uses your phone lines." Sadie leafed through a rail of costumes, each one more showstopping and bombastic than the last, covered in sequins, glass beads, or fine, hand-embroidered artwork. Beyond the corridor, on the other side of the thick velvet curtain, Astrid's band began to warm up, tuning against each other in a cacophonous racket. "Are the lines upstairs connected to the business residence?" Sadie asked.

"No, I'm not as much of an empty suit as some may think," Astrid shot back, returning to her makeup. "The lines aren't connected, but I'll be careful regardless. How long has this been going on?"

Sadie slid the hangers back along the rail until they were all in place once more. "A few weeks, perhaps. It may have started right when Fiske went missing."

"Please, he's not missing, he's dead," Astrid snapped, drawing a neat black line along her eyelashes. "That man enjoyed the limelight far too much and far too often to have developed a taste for solitude."

Sadie tugged another hanger across the rail with a quiet screech, stopping at a black lace bodysuit with rhinestones studded along the sweetheart neckline and traveling up the satin straps. "Regardless, they are making a play for you, Astrid. I highly doubt that Fiske being dead or missing matters much to the prosecution."

"And what are my odds?" Astrid asked, turning back towards the mirror with a huff. "Will I be indicted?"

"That's hard to say without more information. They're grasping at straws here, but Ms. Frost, you need to make certain there aren't any straws left to grasp, am I making myself clear?"

Astrid rolled her eyes at the mirror, knowing Sadie would see anyway. "There was a rumor of another—catering—supplier, but that hasn't turned up anything of value." She swiped black liner across her eyelid, positioned perfectly on the first try. "But yes, fine, I will refrain from trying to source more *forks* for the foreseeable future."

"It is for the best, Ms. Frost," Sadie reiterated. "Caution and prudence will certainly help keep your club open and you out of a jail cell."

"So you don't think the upstairs lines are tapped?" Astrid prompted.

"I can't know for certain," Sadie replied, dragging the black lace aside to reveal a forest green satin corset, adorned with embroidered vines that dipped temptingly from one cup down over the waist and hip. "Is that a liability?"

"It might be," Astrid admitted. "Though it's hard to say. I don't think too much about where I'm placing a call from when I'm unaware that I'm being tapped."

"Which is why I came as soon as I knew." Sadie slid the wires back along the rail, resetting the costumes where she'd first found them. Whoever Astrid's seamstress was, she was very talented. If Sadie didn't know better, she would have guessed that they were Fae-made. "I will liaise with my contacts to get an idea of who they are planning to call as a witness."

"No, no," Astrid protested, tossing her liner down onto the counter with a noisy clatter. "There's no use. It will be too late by then, anyway."

"It could give me an idea of their strategy if this goes to trial."

"I would rather it didn't go to trial."

Sadie resisted the urge to laugh, swallowing it back with an indelicate cough. "Yes, of course, Ms. Frost, no one wants this going to trial."

"You get more money in billable hours if we do," Astrid challenged.

"I wouldn't keep many clients if I played that game," Sadie shot back, her incredulous irritation apparent in her barbed tone. "I aim to keep my clients out of prison so that they can need me again in a few months, not in five to seven years when their appeal finally hits some judge's docket."

Astrid sighed again, but this time it was demure, delicate, and all for show. She was getting ready to perform, shifting gears from shrewd businesswoman and club owner to coquettish siren, ready to preen and seduce her way to an impressive bank balance. "Do what you need to, Ms. Sinclair, but keep me out of trouble and for the love of shadows, out of the hot seat. I don't want to wind up testifying, not even on my own behalf."

"Of course, Ms. Frost."

"There would be far too many invasive questions, and those would likely invite the destruction of this little house of cards." Astrid stood, checking the seams of her hose in the back and straightening the one that was off-center. "And I like my house of cards the way it is. Contrary to popular perception, I'm more of a homebody. The only club I like is my own. That goes the same for company, with very few exceptions." She caught Sadie's eye in the mirror and stared, unflinching. "That is your cue to leave, Ms. Sinclair. I have a show to do. You're welcome to stay if you like. It's hardly a packed house without access to certain musical amplifiers, if you catch my drift."

"I've never understood musical terms, Ms. Frost," Sadie replied, sliding the entire rack to the side of the room, the costumes swaying from their wire hangers, the edges crocheted with pink cotton to keep the straps from slipping. "I will, however, do my best to keep you out of cuffs."

"I prefer the diamond variety." Astrid slipped several sparkling bracelets over her hands, arranging them to show off the delicacy of her wrist bones. "Iron never did anyone any favors, did it?" She grabbed the green satin off of the rail, tugging it on over her underthings, all while maintaining eye contact with such an intense ferocity that Sadie could only wonder what it was Astrid knew. "Do what you need to do, but keep it quiet. I don't need for the prosecutors to think I'm running scared. As far as they are concerned, I would prefer that their image of me as an air-headed jazz singer remain untainted."

"Understood," Sadie confirmed. "I will employ a great deal of discretion." She brushed a hand against the counter, coming away with pink pigment on her fingers from the plush puff that had exploded powder across the varnished wood. "May I ask who your seamstress is?"

"No," Astrid replied, checking her reflection one last time. "You may not." She tightened the straps of the green satin corset, shimmying herself into place as she kept an eye on her reflection. "I expect that you will be gone by the time I return, Ms. Sinclair. I have plans post-show that don't involve uncomfortable conversations with my attorney."

"I have no intention of lingering," Sadie replied, trying to tamp down the irritation in her voice. "I just wanted to warn you that you are being targeted, and I doubt that they will let up any time soon. Tapping the phones is only one part of their plan, and I don't think we want to find out what the next step is. We need to deal with these concerns right now, not wait for you to be indicted."

"How long do I need to make sure this place stays tidy?" Astrid asked, heading for the staircase that led to the stage door. "And how can I know when it's safe?"

"When the case is dismissed," Sadie replied. "We can't let this get past an evidentiary hearing, because any grand jury would delight in sending you to trial. You're a well-to-do mythic with a thriving business, and there are many people in Verdance who would love to make an example of you."

Astrid stiffened, all trace of her coy flirtation evaporated into the artificially dry air, all moisture sucked out by the radiator turned on full blast. "I am plenty aware of what this city likes to do to mythics," she said evenly, despite the twinge of fear wavering at the edges of her tone. "Thank you for the warning, Ms. Sinclair. Not every attorney would go out of their way. Were you followed?"

"No, I made sure of that."

"Good." Astrid nodded, twisting the doorknob and pushing out onto the landing between floors. "It's why I trust you more than the rest of those jokers to keep me out of prison." She cast a glance back towards Sadie, part warning, and part terror. "I can't go to prison, Ms. Sinclair. Women like me don't fare well down in federal."

"Take my advice for the next month or so, and don't deviate from your delivery schedule—" Sadie stopped, following her down the stairs. "You can't get any extra deliveries, Ms. Frost. It would not be prudent to overstock when business is not as bountiful. I guarantee that certain parties are watching."

"The VCPD?"

Sadie nodded. "Yes. They'll have someone staked out, perhaps even in your club."

"Get me that investigator, Ms. Sinclair, Clementine. If someone is trying to throw me underneath the wheels of the train that's speeding towards us, I want to know about it, so that I can deal with them appropriately."

Sadie stayed on the fourth step up from the stage door, not wanting to get too close. Speaking in court was one thing, being on stage was quite another. "I'll do my best, but you might want to consider hiring your usual investigator. She knows what goes on here more than Clementine will, and—"

"No," Astrid interrupted. "That is a foregone conclusion. Vee is uninterested in taking any work from me right now, she's too busy pouting or pining or whatever it is that she's doing." She peeked out the stage door, surveying the room. "Another night of half-full seats," she murmured, shaking her head. "At this rate, it's going to be curtains for this place in a few months. Get the investigator. Find out why it's me they're coming after, and get this shut down." She pasted on a smile, grinning from ear to ear. "I'd hate to take my business elsewhere."

\#

Chapter Eight

Morning came too soon for Sadie's liking. The beams of wintery sun shot through the blinds, drawing stripes along the hardwood floor in even parallels, disturbed only by Sadie's shadow as it dragged behind her. Despite being awake all night, searching for some kind of strategy, digging through law precedents, and drinking enough birch tea to float a barge down the Verdance River, she was going to be late to the office.

She tugged on a fresh pair of slacks, a dark houndstooth charcoal with a matching blazer, and a white shirt fresh from the cleaners, recently pressed, the starch smell still apparent at the collar. Sadie pinned silver points to her collar on either side, attached in the center with a matching chain.

The cab to the office was uneventful, so much so that she was surprised when the ride was over. She stuffed a wad of bills into the driver's hand as she climbed out into the back alley behind her law office. She was uncomfortable with the idea that someone might be watching her and tracking her movements, even if she wasn't the one on trial.

"Morning!" Ella chirped, leaning against her desk in a dark grey wool dress with sleeves to the elbow and a wide belt at her waist. "Hey, would you look at that," she said, motioning between their outfits as Sadie hung up her coat. "Twins!"

"Is that new?" Sadie asked, trying to focus her mind on the quality of the fabric, and not the gentle curve of Ella's hips.

"It is." Ella gave her a little twirl, laughing as she grew dizzy and braced against the filing cabinet for stability. "Do you like it?"

"I do," Sadie said. "It's very nice."

Ella beamed. "I made it!"

"I didn't know you sewed." Despite her affection for Ella, she was incapable of ignoring the slightly uneven stitching along the hemline and the gentle puckering at the left dart. "You're very talented."

"I thought I should start looking more serious if I'm going to be a paralegal." Ella waved her off, holding up a brown paper bag. "Breakfast," she said. "Coffee is percolating."

"What would I do without you?" Sadie asked again, taking the bag from her. She could smell the rich temptation of cinnamon and sugar even through the bag. "Did you beat the crowds today?"

"I wanted one of those cinnamon buns," Ella admitted sheepishly. "It's just as much for selfish enjoyment as it is to bribe you into giving me a raise."

"You don't need to bribe me," Sadie offered. "If you want a raise after you pass your exam, you'll get one."

"I didn't mean it like that, Say," Ella replied quietly. "I was just making a joke."

Sadie repressed the syllables lost in her throat. "I know. I just didn't sleep well last night." She sat in her chair, opening the bag with her eyes closed to fully appreciate the delicious scent emanating from within.

Ella nodded, pouring two large cups of steaming coffee. She dumped six tablespoons of cream into her own, followed by sugar, but delivered Sadie's to her desk unimpeded by adulterating flavors. "I could tell," she replied. "Hey, did you hear there was another body found, this one out on the east side?"

"No," Sadie admitted, sipping at the piping-hot coffee, grateful for its warmth against the frigid bitterness of a late winter morning in Verdance. "Who was it this time?"

"Local business man. No leads, according to the headlines." Ella sat back at her desk, looking in through Sadie's open door. "Cops are saying it looks accidental, maybe an overdose."

"Funny that he could find what he was looking for, and not Astrid," Sadie mused. "Where there's a will, there's a way, I suppose."

"It's just sad, isn't it?" Ella asked. "Seems like this city gets worse every day." Ella shook her head as she took another chunk out of the pastry. "That stuff causes nothing but trouble." She crumpled up the paper bag and depositing it in the can beneath her desk.

The door jingled, announcing the presence of a short, slickly dressed man in navy pinstripes and an ivory wool fedora, already offering up a broad smile. "Good morning," he said smoothly. "I'm looking for representation."

"You've come to the right place," Ella replied, beaming. She dusted the crumbs from her hasily eaten breakfast into the wastebasket beneath her desk and settled the mug of coffee into the upper lefthand corner, the handle facing askew to the decorative wooden molding. "What seems to be the problem, Mr...?"

"Harrow," he supplied, sitting in the chair next to Sadie. "Heincrich is the name."

Ella nodded, pulling a small stack of forms from the filing cabinet behind her. "A pleasure," she said. "This is Ms. Sadie Sinclair, our lead attorney."

Only attorney, Sadie thought as she stood from the chair, feeling strange about the seating arrangement. "Hello, Mr. Harrow," she said, watching as Ella haded him a fresh pen to fill out the forms with, the carbon copies beneath lined up perfectly. "Are you seeking representation for a specific matter, or are you hoping to retain an attorney?"

"Bit of this, bit of that," he said, waving a hand in the air. "You know how it is, Ms. Sinclair, you never know when you'll be in the wrong place at the wrong time."

"Mm," Sadie demurred, tilting her head just enough that it may have looked like a nod of agreement. "You're hoping to retain an attorney, then?" she pressed. "Ms. Beaufort can assist you with—"

"Well, yes and no—what did you say your name was again?" he asked, craning his neck to look at the door. "Ms. Sinclair, that's right, my apologies. You were recommended by Ms. Zin over at the public library, but all I managed to remember was the address."

Ella tapped the top of a form with her pen, drawing his attention back to the paperwork. "If you don't mind, sir, we should have you sign everything before we discuss any of your personal legal issues."

"Oh, it's nothing too exciting," he said, signing his name with a dramatic flourish at the bottom of the page. "A little bit of fraud, they say. Since when is it illegal to mis-balance your accounts? A few bounced checks and the prosecutor wants to treat you like a hardened criminal."

Sliding another page across the desk, Ella began to assemble the man's file. "Have you been arrested?" she asked, straightening the papers lengthwise. "Are you awaiting trial?"

"No," he answered, one hand on each arm rest of the chair, leaning back easily into the seat. "No, I haven't been arrested, I just worry about a few folks coming after me, you know how it is, don't you, Ms. Sinclair?"

Something about the man's demeanor unsettled Sadie, despite his unmistakable human ancestry. She tilted her head again, hoping that her discomfort would read more like professional stoicism than arrogance.

"Anyway, I figure it might be best time to get myself some legal representation. I have some business to attend to coming up pretty soon, and with people unfairly gunning for me, I want to be sure I don't spend more time in lockup than I have to. Are you a round-the-clock firm?" he asked.

Sadie nodded in earnest this time, trying to pull herself back to the job at hand. "Yes, the operator re-routes out-of-office calls to my home address," she explained. "There is a surcharge for that, you understand. Pulling my secretary out of bed in the middle of the night does incur a cost."

"Of course, of course," he said, resting the pen against the second page as the ink bled through to the carbon copies beneath. "It's good that you offer that service, cost or no cost. No one wants to spend time with the old iron bars, do they?"

Sadie flinched, and didn't quite manage to catch herself before she did. Heinrich Harrow squinted at her, leaning forward in the chair as though he was trying to see through her half-human facade. "No, Mr. Harrow, they do not." The sound of her own voice was strangely detached, and wavering at the edges. Ella shot her a look of concern, but Sadie ignored it, reflexively tucking hair over her ears once more. The memory of iron bars was enough to unsettle her, even in passing conversation, and she resented that fact.

"What's the matter, Ms. Sinclair?" he asked. "You done time, or something? Spent a little time downstate?"

The file was cold and smooth in her hands, but Sadie wasn't entirely sure how it got there. Given the look on Ella's face, she must have picked it up off the desk from in front of them both. "I'm so sorry, Mr. Harrow," Sadie said evenly. "Our docket is just too full to take on another retained client at the moment. My deepest apologies, I'd forgotten about another contract we signed just yesterday afternoon, it's unfortunately going to take a great deal of my time."

"So you won't represent me?" he asked, incredulous. "Since when do lawyers turn down work?"

"I prefer to have a manageable client list," Sadie explained. She scribbled the names of a few decent attorneys on a slip of paper, handing it over. "Any one of these will be excellent representation for you, the man at the top of that list has a considerable amount of experience with financial crimes specifically."

Heinrich Harrow stood, but lingered, staring at Sadie. "So much for recommendations," he grumbled. "You might want to tell that librarian friend of yours to keep mum about you if you're not taking on clients."

"I do apologize," Sadie repeated, holding a hand out towards the door. He exited the office, the tails of his coat flapping in the wind.

"What was that all about?" Ella asked when the door latched.

"I don't think I have the time for a financial crimes case," Sadie explained, hoping the lie would be enough. "Not with a man like that, who clearly spends more time in trouble than out of it."

#

Lunch came and went without a fuss, and without actually eating anything. Sadie tapped her fingertips against the polished wood of her desk, passing her break time with worry and irritation instead of with rest and relaxation. Some things remained the same, regardless of which realm she was resident in.

"Hey," Ella said, opening the office's front door and shaking off the dusting of powdery snow that had settled on the shoulders of her thick wool overcoat. "How was lunch?"

"I didn't eat," Sadie replied, setting the files aside for the first time in hours. "How was yours?"

"Ray took me to that little place two streets over," Ella answered. "Sorry I'm late, they were in the middle of a rush."

"Of course, don't worry," Sadie said, offering her a smile despite the unease that was still prickling within her somewhere. She'd hoped that five years in Verdance would have soothed her anxieties about home, but they'd only developed longer shadows.

"Any news while I was gone?" Ella asked, hanging up her coat.

"No, it's been quiet in the office since Mr. Harrow left." The glare of windshields in the winter sun grabbed her attention, and three squad units parked out in front of the office. "Ella, quick," she said, drawing herself to a strict posture. "Get everything back into the cabinet. Don't leave anything out, they'll be looking around at anything they can see."

True to form, Ella didn't hesitate or ask questions, she just did it, and fast. Files got thrown back into their places, and the drawer clicked into place just as the door swung open.

"I'm looking for a Sadie Sinclair, Esquire," said a tall, handsome police captain with a voice like smoky butterscotch. She took up almost the entire doorway with her broad shoulders and muscled figure.

"I hope you have a warrant, Captain," Sadie replied, standing up from her desk. "Or at least, I assume that's why you're here, and not because you are in desperate need of representation."

"Captain Lindell, deputy sheriff," she introduced herself, but didn't extend a hand in greeting. "It's come to my attention that you are Astrid Frost's attorney."

"Yes." Sadie knew better than to offer the cops anything more than the absolute bare minimum, because they'd do anything they could to twist it into evidence.

"The State's Attorney has some concerns about your practice," Captain Lindell said easily, motioning for three other officers behind her to follow into the small office. "I'm here to give you the opportunity to offer up some information before anything escalates."

Sadie smiled, sliding her hands into her pockets. "How kind of you, Captain."

"I'm sure you are aware of the new law in Congress," the captain continued. "If Ms. Frost is indicted, which she likely will be, you could be on the hook as a material witness in her prosecution."

Sadie edged out from behind her desk. "I'm sorry that you have come by some misleading information," she said. "That law has not yet passed through Congress."

"It will, in a matter of days, Ms. Sinclair," the captain pressed, looming over Sadie like a volcano about to erupt. "And when it does, you will be held liable in Ms. Frost's legal indiscretions regarding the distribution and use of illegal substances."

"The law has not yet passed," Sadie said again. "As such, my client Ms. Frost and I still have access to attorney-client privilege, a legally protected right. I can show you her retainer agreement, Captain, if you wish to confirm that she is indeed my client."

"You won't be able to hide behind attorney-client privilege soon, not in matters of national security, which the Nether trade is now classified as, or hadn't you heard?" the captain asked. "I would have thought an attorney of your... reputation, shall we say, would have known all about it." The captain folded her arms over her chest, and the three cops behind her followed suit.

"And I would have thought that a captain of *your* reputation would be wise enough to act on existing law, not proposed law." Sadie picked up the receiver of the phone on her desk and began to dial, dragging the rotary back and forth over the numbers.

"Who are you calling?" Captain Lindell demanded, reaching for the phone cord. "This isn't a game, Ms. Sinclair, this is serious."

"It's none of your business who I am calling, Captain," Sadie replied smoothly, registering a change in her heart rate. "I am not under arrest, nor do you have a warrant, is that correct?"

The captain rested her hand against her service revolver, leaning forward over Sadie's desk. "I can get one in about twenty minutes from a supportive judge," she warned. "And I can guarantee you that if that happens, you won't like the results."

"I admire your optimism, Captain." Sadie said.

"Because I can't imagine that someone like you would last that long in a state correctional facility," the captain warned.

Sadie shuddered again, her skin still prickling with the thought of the blisters they would evoke. She shook the flinch into a nonchalant shrug, pairing it with an gracious smile. "Hello, may I please speak to Judge Liesse?" she asked into the receiver. "Or Judge Haber, if he's available. It's a matter of urgency."

The line crackled with static as the bewildered worker waited for more instructions that made sense, but none came. "Ma'am, this is a deli on Fifth Avenue," they said. "I think you might have the wrong number."

"Yes, thank you, please tell her that a Captain Lindell, deputy sheriff of the VCPD is currently in my office using intimidation tactics to coerce information from me." Sadie covered the receiver and grinned up at the captain. "I'm sorry, Captain, is there a problem?" she asked innocently. Sadie spoke into the receiver once again, despite the employee's protestations. "Yes, thank you, the same office that she visited the last time we met. Thank you. Goodbye."

Captain Lindell folded her arms over her chest, taking her hand away from the holster at her hip. "I should have known you would have seedy connections with a judge," she seethed.

"Please, Captain, do not make the error of assuming that we would all stoop to your level," Sadie said evenly.

"This isn't over, Ms. Sinclair," the captain cautioned. "We will see each other again."

Chapter Nine

Night sank heavily in Verdance, the twilight clouds weighted as they fell towards the earth. Sun set eagerly over a grey horizon, illuminating the thick clouds that had spent all day obscuring the difference between light and dark. Sadie had sent Ella home early, not long after Captain Lindell and her band of merry miscreants had been unceremoniously shooed away from the premises thanks to a mis-dialed number.

The safety of that wouldn't last, in fact, she was surprised that it had held even for a few hours. It wouldn't take long for word to travel from Lindell to whoever her friendly judge was, back to Judge Liesse, who may or may not appreciate Sadie dropping her name into the mess. Angering a judge in Verdance was inadvisable, to say the least.

Of course, as soon as the officers left, Sadie spent the rest of the afternoon and evening poring over files, searching for anything that could cause problems for her mythical clients. While Senator Dean's law had yet to pass, it would, and Captain Lindell would be back with more questions, a warrant, and she'd be followed by a subpoena for Sadie's records and files on every mythic suspected of Nether use. Given the growing ubiquity of the drug, that would be nearly half the mythics that found themselves in legal trouble. If the government and the police departments found themselves in lockstep with their respective overreach, she'd have to work even harder to protect her clients.

Sadie scoured three stacks of files before she allowed herself to lean back in her chair, half-starved and exhausted from the day. The golden light from her desk lamp pooled over varnished wood and the lightly crumpled edges of case files, some of them years old. There were three drawers left to go before she could go home for the night, because if that law passed in the morning, Captain Lindell would be back by lunch. Sadie had come too far to lose her reputation as an advocate, had worked too hard and too long to lose what little she'd built in the human realm. The thought of home pulled at her, gently at first and then more insistent with the purple-pink glow from the mirror when she caught herself looking. She couldn't go back, not when it would be the ruination of her people.

"No," she said aloud to the empty office. "I'm not giving up." Sadie flipped open the next file, a case from three years back, a slip and fall involving a home goods storefront and a shifter down on his luck. They'd won, but only after Sadie had proved that the store had been warned at least four times by the city to repair the leak from the gutter. They'd tried to bury the records, but she'd found them just the same. She hadn't spent all that time in the Fae archives practicing the patience of the search for nothing.

File after file, case after case, she searched. The potential new federal law about Nether distribution was threatening to drag her under, too, and she knew that Astrid Frost would let it happen, so long as she stayed out of hot water. Women like Astrid surrounded themselves with flunkies who'd happily take the fall. She'd defended one of them four years back after being charged with distribution to keep Astrid out of hot water.

That was the next file she opened, the one for Virginia Vane. Her mug shot stared back at Sadie, sharp cheekbones, scars that dragged over one eye, and a look that could kill. Sadie would be surprised if the photographer had survived it. Virginia Vane may as well have been a gorgon for how unapproachable she was, not wanting to give even one shred of extra evidence or alibi that would help her case, because it might have implicated Astrid instead.

The felt tip screeched in protest as she dragged it across the page's edge to indicate it had already been scoured. There hadn't been anything to find yet, although she did shred two documents relating to undocumented mythics. They were both seers, desperate to avoid conscription.

Sadie groaned, closing the file. There wasn't much left in it after the removal of both pages, and she worried that the VCPD would notice that something was amiss. A warrant could uncover the seers she'd helped keep hidden.

She couldn't help but let her thoughts drift to eating something hot and fried at her desk. If there was anything the human realm did better, it was food. They weren't afraid to fry things, to desecrate the simple beauty of fresh vegetables, tubers, and bread with the gorgeous hedonism of hot oil. It was three in the morning, too late to bother going home to sleep, not when she'd have to be back at six-thirty to ward off Captain Lindell, and there were still more files to search.

There was an all-night diner just four blocks away. She could run in, get takeout, and be back in twenty minutes. Without food, she might collapse over on her desk, and Ella would find her in the morning, half-starved, exhausted, and useless. Humans loved to think themselves invincible, even though they were more mortal than most. The Fae spent half their time in court, and the other half in recreation. Humans, especially those in Verdance, spent all their time toiling, suffering, and depriving themselves, wondering why everything in their lives felt so dull and hollow.

Sadie felt faint as she stood up from the desk, wobbling slightly on her feet from hunger. She'd never been very good at hunger. It ate at her, dissolving her from the inside out, and in the human realm, it was inescapable. The night was quiet, undisturbed by the VCPD, the feds, clients, or the imposition of traffic. Twenty minutes, that's all it would take, and then she'd power through until morning. She'd thank herself with an early night and a mug of weak birch tea, so long as she managed to protect her clients—and herself—a little while longer.

\#

When Sadie returned to the office, steaming boxes of takeout in her hands, she unlocked the door and placed them onto the side table, her constitution weak with the protest that she hadn't broken open the boxes on the walk home. The only reason she hadn't was the frigid night temperature, which would have sapped any warmth in no time at all. She couldn't abide cold food.

The files she'd left on her desk had been disturbed.

She froze, positioning the key between her knuckles as if it would do anything against the threat of a gun. Beyond her office door, someone shuffled in the darkness, the scrape of boot leather against the beveled edge of the wood.

Green eyes flashed in the darkness, along with the silver glint of metal. Sadie jerked to the side, holding the chair between her and her would-be attacker. Blood pounded in her ears as she tried to recount everyone who would possibly wish her harm. Much to her chagrin, the list was longer than she could parse in the limited seconds available.

"Relax, Ms. Sinclair, it's just me."

Sadie squinted, her eyes finally adjusting to the lack of light, but the revelation didn't do much to comfort her. "Ms. Vane," she said, clearing her throat. "What a surprise, I heard you were out of town."

The private investigator stared back at her, unmoving. "I'm not."

"May I ask why you're here in my office so early?"

Virginia Vane stood up from Sadie's desk, folding her hands back into the pockets of her sleek overcoat, perfectly tailored to her shape. "The feds are after Astrid. You can tell her I let you know that."

"I'm aware," Sadie replied. "She was subpoenaed." She kept hold of the chair, always intimidated by Virginia's terrible iciness. Most people were easy to read. She wasn't. "If they put you on the stand, they may well mention the John Warren murder."

"I assumed as much," Virginia said. "I told them I wouldn't testify, and if they forced the issue, I'd act as a hostile witness. You can tell her that, too."

"They will force you to testify, regardless," Sadie warned.

Virginia shrugged lightly. "I would imagine so."

"The VCPD was here today. A Captain Lindell showed up with three squad units." Sadie picked up her takeout, reaching around Virginia. "May I offer you some?"

"No thank you," Virginia answered, more politely than Sadie might have imagined she would. "Captain Lindell was here?"

"Yes, with indications that she intends to return with a warrant as soon as that law is passed." Sadie pried open the paper box, letting loose a thin rivulet of steam that floated up toward the ceiling and dissipated before it ever met the tiles. "Which is why I'm here at nearly four in the morning. What is unclear, is why you are."

Virginia straightened her tie, and did it without even checking her reflection in the glass of the picture frame to her left. "I was in the neighborhood," she explained. "What's the likelihood they'll get this warrant after that law is passed in the next few days?"

"Very," Sadie responded. "Nothing in my files suggests any wrongdoing on Astrid's part, but I don't want the VCPD or the feds in here rifling through my casework. I imagine you of all people understand why that is."

"I do," Virginia said with a nod. "How did you get rid of them?"

"Ah, it was a case of assumptions on Captain Lindell's part, and an unfortunate mis-dial to the local deli."

Virginia exhaled a laugh through her nose. "I bet Shirin loved that," she muttered.

"Shirin?" Sadie prompted.

"Captain Lindell. Listen, Ms. Sinclair, keep your nose out of trouble and try not to piss off the cops, alright?" Virginia glanced at the box of food, tilting her head to the side. "Where did you get that from?"

"Jen's diner, four blocks east," Sadie replied. "Best fried cheese in Verdance that can be had in the middle of the night."

"A rousing endorsement," Virginia replied. "Tell Astrid I tried to warn her."

"Is there a reason you can't tell Ms. Frost that yourself?" Sadie asked, curious but knowing well enough not to pry.

"Aside from the fact that they're almost certainly tapping her phones and I have no interest in getting hauled into VCPD headquarters for questioning, I also have no interest in talking to Astrid." Virginia came around to the other side of the desk, dragging her hand across the wood, the silver knuckles on her hand grating against varnish. "But I don't want her bringing trouble to my door, either."

"I'll ensure that she is made aware."

"You do that." Virginia clapped her on the shoulder as she passed, sidling between the chairs to exit into the reception area.

"Wait," Sadie said, remembering both her promise to Astrid and the gala. "I need something from you. It's… sensitive."

Virginia raised an eyebrow, the scars over her face shining in the dim light from the street lamp outside the door. "I'm listening."

"There's another investigator in Verdance, a Clementine Dorefield," Sadie explained, setting down her food. She swept up the files from the chair, setting them into the nearest filing cabinet. "I need to know more about her, and if she's looking into me."

"What am I looking for?" Virginia asked. "Affairs, debts? Are you trying to hire her or get rid of her?"

"Get rid?" Sadie echoed.

"Get her off your tail," Virginia replied, rolling her eyes.

"Yes I would prefer she left me alone, but I don't wish her ill."

Virginia shrugged. "Bad things happen to people all the time." She pulled at the doorknob, letting in a gust of fine flakes dislodged from the awning. "This is favor for favor. No invoices, no receipts. It's frowned upon for investigators to look too deeply into each other. We have a code."

"Yes, a favor," Sadie agreed. "I could make myself available to you for legal advice, should the need arise again."

"I'll let you know when it comes up." Virginia stepped out into the black morning, the sun barely bleeding rays at the horizon. "And make sure you tell Astrid what I said."

Chapter Ten

Sadie was leaned back in her chair, drifting in and out of a restless sleep when Ella floated through the door, setting her packed lunch on the desk with the crinkle of a paper bag.

"Say?" she called through the door, a note of alarm in her voice. "What are you doing here?"

"Pre-spring cleaning," Sadie replied, flourishing a gesture towards the filing cabinets. "I went through everything, in case Captain Lindell shows up with a warrant this time."

Ella started to throw things into Sadie's briefcase, three files, notepads, and a pen. "Sadie, you're supposed to be in court!" she chastised, thrusting the case over the desk. "Don't you remember? You have a hearing with Judge Haber!"

"*Kelvaris.*" Sadie breathed a Fae curse under her breath like a hex, practically catapulting herself out of her chair. "No, I forgot, I thought it was still Tuesday." She checked her watch, eyes still adjusting to consciousness. "I'm already late?"

"You'd better hurry, or he's going to have your guts for garters." Ella stopped her at the door, smoothing wrinkles from her blazer and straightening the lapels. "There. You look ravishing."

"I'm not sure that ravishing is going to save me from being held in contempt," Sadie said, but Ella's compliment rang brightly in her ears. At the thought, she checked her hair, finding it still secured. "Which case? Is it the wrongful termination?"

"Yes," Ella confirmed, nudging her towards the door. "Eat the muffin I put in there, you're not at your best when you don't eat. It's bran, sorry. All they had left."

"It's better than nothing." Sadie wished she'd disposed of the previous night's—well, morning really—takeout containers that had collected on her desk. Nary a crumb was left, but leaving evidence at all of being disorganized was an anathema to her. "Thank you," she said, and meant it.

"Hurry!" Ella urged, shooing her towards the door.

Sadie shot out into the cold morning, pulling her blazer tight around her shoulders. She was already five minutes late, and court was a ten-minute drive without traffic, twenty in rush hour. She checked her watch for a third time, blinking blearily at the glare from the winter sun off the face, and hissed out a sigh. She had no choice but to drive, and so she climbed into the driver's side and thrust the key into the ignition, cursing herself for falling asleep and cursing herself for not heading home or setting an alarm. She'd forgotten the hearing. It was a pro-bono case, which of course made her feel even guiltier about the fact that it had slipped her mind.

Traffic crawled, and then it surged, and she was throwing the car into park before it had even come to a complete stop. She glided with elongated, rushed strides through the marble-floored halls of the state courthouse. She burst through the door, apologies ready on her tongue, but the judge held up his hands to silence her.

"You're late, Ms. Sinclair," he chastised.

"Yes, I'm sorry, Your Honor." Sadie knew not to make excuses, it would only make him angrier. "I'm here now, and I apologize sincerely for the delay."

He held the gavel aloft, his face twisted into a soured frown as he decided how harshly to punish her. "This is a pro-bono case, is it not?"

"It is," she confirmed, sweeping through the half-height swinging doors to take her place at the table. "And I apologize to opposing counsel." She glanced at who it was and winced. It was Betty Coleman, a well-known shark on the Verdance law scene. "Ms. Coleman," she said politely, nodding her head. "Good to see you again."

"I wonder where Ms. Sinclair was last night that she couldn't manage to be on time today," Betty murmured under her breath, not quite loud enough for the judge to hear.

The judge cleared his throat, taking a stack of files from the bailiff. "I understand this is a suit filed to protest wrongful termination?" he asked, shuffling through the paperwork.

"It is, Your Honor," Sadie confirmed. She turned to her client, offering him a reassuring smile. Given the twisted reflection in the black marble column, she knew that all she had achieved was grotesque. "Mr. Araday was terminated from his position as a security guard at the Third National Bank without cause."

Judge Haber nodded, settling the pair of tiny spectacles on his nose. "Ms. Coleman?" he prompted, clearing his throat.

"It is my client's position that Mr. Araday was fired for cause," Betty replied, smoothing the front of her crisp ivory skirt. "We would make a motion to dismiss, Your Honor, as we have irrefutable proof that Mr. Araday has no claim in this case."

"Objection," Sadie refuted, still standing. "That has yet to be determined, Ms. Coleman."

"Let's all take a deep breath, shall we?" Judge Haber suggested, setting down his gavel. "I'm sure we can all manage to keep this civil."

Betty gave him a huge, fake smile that was plastered across her perfectly blushed cheeks. "Of *course*, Your Honor," she assured him in a demure tone that she'd never use outside of court.

"*Fantastic*," Sadie breathed with quiet irritation. She straightened, opening the file from her briefcase, the bran muffin staring at her temptingly from within. "Your Honor, my client was never once written up for any infractions, and his quarterly reviews were always glowing." She slipped the documents out of their folder, giving a copy to Betty, and one to the judge. "Here we have his performance record, and as you can see, he was well-regarded by his colleagues, and praised regularly by his supervisor."

"Objection, Your Honor, we have never seen these documents," Betty protested. "How are we to prepare our case if we aren't made aware of evidence?"

Sadie resisted the urge to laugh and pointed at the letterhead. "These documents were sourced from your client, ma'am, they have been made aware of their existence, because they are the ones who created them."

"Then I have to be blunt, Your Honor, these documents are not accurate." Betty stood, shoulders delicately squared as she tugged her papers free of their file. "This is a sworn affidavit from Mr. Araday's former employer, who wanted to let us know that he was terminated from his position as a bouncer at the Sphinx nightclub for using excessive force with their patrons."

Swallowing back the growl that was growing in her throat, Sadie turned to her client with a questioning lock. He shrugged back at her and shook his head. "Ms. Coleman, this seems terribly convenient, don't you think?" Sadie suggested. Of course Astrid had made a deal with someone to keep the heat low. Of course she hadn't said anything, either, and of course, she'd done all of it in less than twenty-four hours. It was just how Astrid worked. "What is the name on the affidavit?" she asked.

"Bryce Callwell," Betty replied.

"Your Honor!" Sadie huffed in exasperation. "How are we to rebut this? Mr. Callwell died six weeks ago, how did he manage to swear an affidavit?"

"As you well know, Ms. Sinclair, this case has been on Judge Haber's docket for two months. We were lucky enough to get this affidavit before Mr. Callwell's untimely death. And as you also should know, given that you passed the bar at the same time I did, that affidavits that have been appropriately notarized don't expire in this state, given the seal has not been tampered with, which His Honor can certainly see for himself." Betty crossed one leg over the other and raised an eyebrow in challenge. She had the power of a top law firm at her back, as well as the funding of the Third National Bank.

"Regardless of my client's past infractions, that should have no bearing on this case," Sadie protested.

"It goes to character," Betty pressed. "It's entirely relevant to this matter."

Judge Haber broke the seal and adjusted his glasses, reading the affidavit. "Ms. Sinclair, I'm afraid your opposing counsel is correct. You are overruled."

Sadie's client tugged at her sleeve, a desperate look on his face. "Please, Ms.

Sinclair," he begged. "My family is counting on me. Without my wages from my job at the bank, they won't be able to keep up with the rent or anything else."

She nodded, the gravity and the weight dragging at her, the same they always did for these kinds of cases. Despite her insistence on payment for everyone else, the most hopeless and desperate managed to tug at her heartstrings. "Your Honor," Sadie began, shuffling through the files and the paperwork that Ella had crammed into her briefcase on the way out the door, each one color-coded and tabbed.

"Yes?" the judge prompted, still twirling the gavel in his hands. "What is it, Ms. Sinclair?"

Sadie smiled up at him, trying to regain any good graces she'd lost in turning up late. "While opposing counsel's submissions are indeed fascinating, my client's record of achievement at Third National Bank is far more relevant than any indiscretions at previous places of employment." She tugged another page free of the file, the paper loose and smooth in her hands. "I would like to submit into evidence this affidavit from Mr. Araday's supervisor on the second shift, indicating that he was never late for work, he showed exemplary improvement in several key areas, and that he was hired because he is a shifter."

"Your Honor!" Betty interjected with an aggrieved gasp, rocketing up out of her chair. "Any affidavit from Mr. Araday's manager should be found moot, as he already agreed to testify for the defense."

Judge Haber tilted his head in one direction, and then the other, as if the shift in perspective would give him the answer he needed. "Is this witness present?" he asked, gesturing around the room.

Betty flattened her palms against the desk. "No, Your Honor, unfortunately, we were unable to locate him in time for court."

"Then, given this affidavit, Ms. Coleman, I would have to assume that this manager changed his mind about which side of this he wants to be on." The judge shrugged lightly, the black cotton robes rising and falling with the motion. "Overruled."

"We would ask to cross-examine this witness," Betty continued. "After all, that is our right as the defense. We ask Your Honor for the opportunity to serve a subpoena to determine the true opinions of this manager. We ask for a continuance until we can locate him."

The judge chewed his lip, twirling the gavel in his hands, the glint of polished wood flashing in the rare spots of sunbeams pressing through the gaps in the thick, velvet curtains. "Motion granted," he said after a moment. "Get your managerial witness in here, and then we'll talk."

"Your Honor," Sadie protested, sidling around her desk, "an affidavit is more than enough to show that Mr. Araday was not derelict in his duties at his workplace. This is a delaying tactic from opposing counsel to keep Third National Bank from having to pay for their legal infractions, and to deny Mr. Araday anything resembling justice."

The courtroom door opened with a quiet whine, revealing none other than Astrid Frost in her fox-fur coat, opened to the waist to reveal the crisply tailored mauve skirt suit, the hem an inch past the knee and probably the most demure thing she'd worn in months. She caught Sadie's eye, shook her head, and took a seat in the last row of the gallery, crossing one leg over the other. Whatever was going on, it was about to become even more of a problem for Sadie than it already was.

Judge Haber watched Astrid as she settled herself onto the bench, adjusting her hat so that the brim laid low over one eye, her waved hair peeking out from underneath. "I, uh..." he trailed off, before shaking his head. "Unfortunately, Ms. Sinclair, your opposing counsel does have the right to rebut testimony, and in light of this other witness—' he paused, looking over his notes. "In light of Mr. Callwell's untimely demise, I think we should allow for as much in-person testimony as possible, don't you think?"

Sadie's jaw clamped, and she breathed out a tightly controlled sigh, the frustration hissing out between her teeth. "Of course, Your Honor," she agreed, despite the red-hot burn of lies snaking its way up her throat. "But I would plead with the court that any delay will only serve to further damage Mr. Araday's finances."

"Agreed," Judge Haber said, nodding over at Betty. "You have one week to track down this witness, Ms. Coleman, or we will proceed with this case. Are we understood?"

"Absolutely," Betty replied brightly, winking over at Sadie. "We will track him down as soon as we get that subpoena."

"Excellent." The judge cracked the gavel against the desk, the sound ricocheting between marble, quartz, and Sadie's ears. Not getting enough sleep always made her want to lock herself in a soundproofed room and never leave. "We will reconvene in one week."

Sadie slid files back into their folders, replacing the tabs that Ella had left. She'd be needing them again in a week, especially if they managed to track down the shift supervisor. They likely wouldn't, because she knew for a fact he'd decided to take a vacation after swearing the affidavit. Clearly, the opposition hadn't figured that part out yet. With any luck, they wouldn't. "It's alright," she soothed, patting her client on the arm. "We'll see justice done. I just know it."

"Thank you, Ms. Sinclair," he said, burying his head in his hands for just a moment before he stood, buttoning his suit jacket, tattered at the hem and cuffs. It was probably a hand-me-down from a brother or a father, but it drove home the need for him to access pay that was rightfully his. "I'm gonna spend a couple of days at my mom's place." He scribbled a number on the top folder and slipped the pen back into his breast pocket. "In case you need to get hold of me."

She nodded, but before she could say anything else, he pushed through the barrier, through the courtroom doors, and he was gone. Everyone was gone by then, except for Astrid, who still sat glowering in the last row.

"Ms. Frost," Sadie said, pausing at the last row. "What a surprise to see you here."

"You know shadows-damned well why I'm here," she spat. "What are you doing defending Araday?"

"It's my business who I represent," Sadie replied easily. "Is there something else you wanted to discuss? If so, you're more than welcome to call the office and make an appointment with Ella, or—"

Astrid stood, leaning in until the stray hairs of her fur coat brushed against Sadie's hand. "Drop the case, Ms. Sinclair," she whispered, the warning loud and clear despite the hushed tone. "It will just be easier for everyone."

Sadie sucked her teeth, resisting the urge to check her hair because Astrid's proximity was more than just a threat, she was a promise of terrible things to come. "Easier for you first and foremost, I imagine," she replied. "Why are you making deals with Third National Bank? Why do something that throws another mythic under the proverbial bus?"

"My business is my own," Astrid stated, not even moving a muscle. Her propensity for perfect, statuesque posture was supremely unnerving, despite her petite frame. "Drop the case."

"Or?" Sadie prompted, adjusting the placement of the files in her arms.

"I take my business elsewhere." Astrid reapplied a fresh coat of deep red lipstick, almost burgundy in shade, maintaining eye contact all the while. "We both know you can't afford to lose me as a client."

Quiet murmurs drifted through the thick, carved doors, indicating that most courts had let out for a lunch recess. "Give me a good reason, then," Sadie offered. "I'm a reasonable attorney, and I am more than happy to accept when I've taken on work I shouldn't have. Tell me why I should drop the case, and I'll consider it."

Astrid stepped back, tossing the tube of lipstick back into her handbag with a flourish indicative of her career. "Third National Bank doesn't want to be setting any dangerous kinds of precedents."

"Like being responsible for their poor management decisions?" Sadie asked, tucking the files back into her bag. "They want to be able to terminate employment based on what, mythic status? And you, as a mythic, are fine with this?"

"Ms. Sinclair, I don't know if you're aware of this, but other people will never watch your back the way you can watch your own." Astrid stepped around her, laying a hand against the door. "My advice to you is to keep a close eye on your own ass, before meddling gets you mixed up with the wrong kinds of people."

\#

\#

Chapter Eleven

Three days passed in a blur of paperwork and two court appearances before Sadie felt like she could come up for air. "Finally," she breathed, sliding the last file into the cabinet.

"All done?" Ella called from the next room, leaning up over her desk to glance into Sadie's office. "Shadows be damned, that took forever."

"Indeed it did," Sadie murmured, resting her forearms against the edge of the desk, the tension in her shoulders frustratingly present. "And you? Are we thoroughly checked?"

Ella nodded, sitting back in her chair, which removed her from view. "I triple-checked everything you did the other night, and I think we're covered if that law passes." There was a quiet pause, in which the only sound was that of papers being shuffled and the jingle of the bakery's bell next door. "Do you think it will?"

"Yes," Sadie admitted. "Senator Jonathan Dean, or J.D. as he insists the papers call him, is only growing in popularity, and so is support for this new law. People have heard too many stories like I heard in court the other day, they want action to be taken when it comes to the issue of Nether."

"And what about Ms. Frost's subpoena??" Ella asked, the legs of her chair squeaking against the hardwood floor. "Do you have any leads? Any idea how to stop the possibility of her being indicted?"

Sadie gave a demure sigh, the weight of it heavy at the top of her spine. "I have to be honest, Ella, I think she's going to lose this round. That witness was very sympathetic, and any grand jury will agree with his testimony." She pulled a notebook from her desk, scanning through her notes on her current cases. "Ms. Frost needs an incredible twist in the case to avoid arrest at this stage."

Before Sadie could expound on her ideas for unearthing evidence that would exonerate Astrid Frost, her office door swung open, and there was Clementine, glaring straight through the office.

"Ms. Dorefield," Sadie said, standing. "How nice to see you again."

"You had me followed?" Clem demanded, positioning one elegant hand against her hip, fingers wrapping around the thick black wool of her overcoat, drumming her fingers silently against the fabric.

Sadie cleared her throat and motioned for Ella to show Clementine into her office. "Why would I have you followed, Ms. Dorefield?" Sadie asked, knowing exactly where the conversation was headed.

"Please, Virginia Vane is about as subtle as a fireworks display," Clem hissed, slamming Sadie's office door behind her. "She thinks she's a good tail, but I saw her coming a mile off."

Sadie sat back down, raising an eyebrow. "It still took you three days of being tailed to figure it out," she said casually. "Sounds like a decent tail to me."

"She wasn't tailing me for three days, she's overcharging you," Clem snapped, but there was an unmistakable waver to her voice that showed her worry and insecurity. "She only started late last night."

"She started three days ago," Sadie corrected. "Does that alarm you?"

"It doesn't alarm me, Ms. Sinclair, it makes me wonder what in shadows you think you're playing at." Clem pressed her hands against the desk, leaning forward to tower over Sadie, to intimidate her, or at the very least to scare her off that particular course of action.

"I was having you vetted," Sadie explained evenly. "Obviously, telling you that would have compromised your natural movements throughout the day."

Clem flinched at the admission, dropping her hands to her sides. "Vetted?" she asked. "For what?"

Sadie smiled broadly, enjoying both the change in Clem's dynamic and the shift in the power differential. "I'm afraid I can't tell you, Ms. Dorefield. It's confidential."

"Confidential," Clem repeated, a flash of rage dancing across the cornflower blue of her irises. "That sounds like bullshit lawyer speak for someone who doesn't want to have their ass handed to them in court."

"Yes, confidential," Sadie repeated. "Sometimes, a client asks me to use my connections and my skills to vet someone, and if I were to disclose that, not only would it be a violation of attorney-client—"

"Okay, I get the idea," Clem seethed. "Tell Vane to stay the hell away from me, alright? I don't like that she's creeping around."

Sadie nodded casually as she sat, folding her hands atop the desk. "I will, as soon as I have her full report."

"You don't yet?" Clem sat, gripping the arms of the chair with pinched knuckles. "When will you?"

"When she's done, I expect." Sadie straightened a pen that had been lying askew at the edge. "Is that all, Ms. Dorefield?"

"How did she find me?"

"I don't know, that's something you'd have to ask her," Sadie answered. "But Ms. Vane doesn't strike me as someone who is overly keen on sharing her methodologies, if I'm honest." She smiled across the desk in challenge, waiting for Clem to say something else vaguely incriminating. "If your vetting was completed without issue, I'm sure I'll be in touch soon with the next steps for this particular contract."

"Strange that you would vet me before making an offer," Clem retorted. "What if I don't have time in my schedule?"

Sadie blinked, letting the ghost of a smile play across her lips. "Then we would simply hire someone else."

"What's the pay?"

"Enough."

Clem exhaled a laugh through her nose, leaning forward against the desk. "Who is to say what is and isn't enough, Ms. Sinclair?" she asked. "My rates might not coincide with what they're offering."

"They will," Sadie responded casually. Astrid's pockets were deep, and she spared no expense when it came to protecting her own assets. "I wouldn't worry about the rate of pay, just that you passed the vetting. Is there anything you're concerned about, that you might want to explain before Ms. Vane comes in with the report?"

"She has a lot of skeletons in her closet, you know," Clem sniped, practically spitting out the words in a vitriolic rush. "Virginia Vane shouldn't be trusted with anything high level, especially vetting."

"I'm aware of her past."

"Is this employer?" Clem challenged. "Does whoever is doing the hiring know that she's a disgraced cop, that she was running Nether for the Ruby Thorns four years back? How about her dalliances with the VCPD, doesn't that raise any alarms?"

Sadie tilted her head. "Your concerns are misplaced. I am more than well aware of Ms. Vane's predilection to trouble, and if you are referring to the distribution charges from four years back, those were dropped due to a woeful lack of evidence." She tapped her pen against the desk, creating an uneven, unsettling rhythm that pierced through the relative silence of the office. "Furthermore, Virginia Vane isn't in the running for this position, you are."

"Because of her past?"

Sadie waited a long moment before she replied. "That's confidential."

"Whatever this investigation job is, let me just tell you something, Ms. Sinclair. Private eyes like Virginia Vane might be effective, but they cut corners." Clem pressed against the desk with her black leather gloved hands, the lambswool peeking out from the cuff. "I don't cut corners. I won't be the reason an investigation goes awry."

"I already told you, she's not in contention," Sadie explained. "You'll know if you passed the vetting when I know, alright?"

Clem shifted uncomfortably in her seat, now tugging at the fingertips of her gloves before pressing them back down. A tell, but a delicate one. "I prefer to keep my work life and my private life separate," she said. "I don't like being followed. We have a code, you know. Investigators. It's not written into law, but the rest of us trying to make a living actually do our best to stay the hell out of whatever drama this city is cooking up. My life is my own, Ms. Sinclair.

If you want information, you can just ask me. I'm an open book."

"Oh, I very much doubt that," Sadie replied. "And if your private life is a problem, you can just tell me now." She held her hands out in a deferential gesture, drawing her shoulders up gently towards her ears. "It's your choice, Ms. Dorefield."

"Just admit that you sent Vane after me because you were angry about the night of the gala," Clem taunted. "Admit it, Sadie, you didn't like that you'd been had by a private investigator, that you didn't know who'd sent me."

"I'm sure I'll find out soon enough." Sadie offered a demure smile, the edges of her lips barely turned upwards. "Was there anything else you needed, Clem?"

"I don't think it's very fair to be vetting me before I've even agreed to take the position," Clem insisted. "And Vane will almost undoubtedly get all the fine details wrong."

Sadie tilted her head to one side, and then the other, taking in the sight of Clem in her coat and suit, the vague pinstripes of her mid-length skirt almost invisible. "You will want this job."

"How do you know?"

"Is working at your law firm really enough for you?" Sadie asked. "How many divorces have you worked on now, Clem? How many unfaithful spouses have you tailed to a motel, just to wait in the parking lot with a camera? How many corporate interests who want you to undermine their competition?" She ran her fingers along the edge of her chair, irritated by the loose thread she found at the join. "The potential intrigue of this case has you interested, Ms. Dorefield."

"Divorces and corporate espionage pay the bills far better than pro-bono cases for mythics," Clem shot back.

Sadie raised an eyebrow, but the rest of her positioning remained the same. "That may be so," she argued. "And yes, most of my clientele are mythics, what does that have to do with anything?"

"Verdance is changing, Ms. Sinclair," Clem retorted in a warning tone. "The entire world is changing, even more now than when The Rupture first happened. It probably won't be long until mythics are barely even citizens anymore. I can't imagine that bodes well for their attorneys."

Sadie studied Clem's face, finding something there that she couldn't quite make out. "I plan to do my best to keep that from happening," she explained. "One case at a time, Ms. Dorefield. Empires weren't built in a day."

"Every other headline these days is about a mythic causing problems," Clem argued. "Public opinions is shifting." She tightened the tie at the waist of her coat, still dusted with snow from the blowing drifts outside. "You should get a clue as to what's happening out there, Ms. Sinclair."

"I'm well aware of the current state of affairs in Verdance," Sadie shot back. "You are invited to leave my office Ms. Dorefield, and as soon as the vetting report is handed over to me, I'll inform you of the findings, and discuss the potential employment."

Clem's eyes narrowed at this, and she stood, gripping the edge of the desk with such force that it jarred Sadie out of her comfortably reclined position. "You have no idea what you're getting into, you know that?" she asked, hand already on the plain brass doorknob. "Absolutely not a single clue rattling around in that very pretty, very empty skull you've got stapled to your shoulders that you're toying with things you shouldn't be messing with. Not when you have no idea what kind of forces are at play."

"Oh?" Sadie asked, taking out her notebook. "And what are these forces?"

"Me," Clem threatened, now bent over the desk and sneering, her face contorted into a snarl that was not befitting of her natural beauty. "Don't have me tailed again, Ms. Sinclair."

"I will let you know when I have Ms. Vane's report," Sadie said after a moment, unable to temper the steely tone to her voice.

"Tell Vane to stay off my tail, or she'll regret it."

\#

Chapter Twelve

Sadie placed her keys into the wire basket on the table with a satisfying jingle and threw the deadbolt. She'd been spending so much time at the office and in court that she'd barely had much time at all for being at home, or sleeping, or eating something that didn't come in a paper box with a handle. Stretching her arms up over her head, she slipped off her thick coat, hanging it on the stand by itself.

She caught her reflection in the window and frowned at what she saw there, dark circles, gaunt cheeks, and a shirt with a bent collar that she definitely should have ironed before leaving the apartment that morning. For someone raised on sartorial propriety, Sadie looked like she'd just been dragged out of bed unceremoniously, through a thick hedge, and offered nothing on the other side of it.

"Honey, I'm home," she said to no one, a private joke that cut her a little more deeply every time an answer didn't echo back in her direction. She tied up her hair on top of her head, relishing the feel of cool air against her ears. She wished she could do so more often, but that would compromise not only her own identity, but the existence of the other realm entirely. Rupture or no Rupture, as far as humankind was concerned, the Fae had died out centuries before.

A knock jarred her from her forlorn reverie, and she froze, one hand on her hair, and the other reaching for the large filleting knife from the block on her quartz countertop.

"Who's there?" she asked, tugging curls down over her ears. Once again, back into hiding. No one ever visited her at home, not even Ella.

Especially not Ella.

Seeing her there would only make Verdance's long winter nights even more unbearable, being able to solidly picture what she'd look like draped across the sofa, or yawning in the morning, arms stretched over her head, or—

The knock interrupted her once more, and with the chain on the door, she cracked it open, holding the knife behind her back in case of an assailant. It wouldn't have been the first time that an aggrieved ex-client had tracked down her home address.

"Ms. Sinclair, you can put down the knife," Virginia said, leaning against the outside door frame. "I'm not going to attack you."

Sadie slid the chain from the door, opening it wider, checking her hair once again, and finding it appropriately demure. "Ms. Vane," she said, relieved that it wasn't anyone else. "No, I'm sorry, of course not."

"If you're worried about security, which I'm guessing you are given the size of that knife, you should consider swapping out your deadbolt. This brand is easier to pick, if you know what you're doing." She passed over a large cream envelope, a red string looped around a closure button. "Here's everything I could find on Clementine Dorefield."

Sadie took the file and tucked it under her arm, wishing to explore the evidence in the privacy of her own mind. "Thank you. She invited herself to my office today. She discovered that you were tailing her."

"She's very good at what she does. I swapped vehicles twice, but she still spotted me," Virginia explained. "I still managed to get three days' worth of intel about who she is, and what she's been up to." She shifted her position, leaning against the door frame on her right forearm, glancing past Sadie into her apartment. "Nice place."

"Thank you," Sadie replied. "It's not in its usual state. I've barely been home lately."

Virginia stared, chewing her lip like she was biting back a comment. She rolled her shoulders back and pushed off the door frame, straightening. "It's my professional opinion that this investigator would be a good choice for this job with Astrid. She's smart, she's intuitive, and less likely to get herself killed or framed than some of the other investigators in Verdance. Clementine Dorefield is seasoned." She nodded towards the file, toying with a tarnished silver cigarette case in one hand, the telltale sign of a chain smoker. "She works with a few different law firms, all top-shelf in Verdance. She's won them plenty of cases, and has a salary to match."

"I appreciate your analysis." A part of Sadie was still burnt and ashen that she'd fallen into bed with Clem in the first place. She shouldn't have, but the crushing weight of independence was too suffocating, some days. "Was there anything else of note?"

"Did you know she's hiding a marriage?" Virginia asked.

Sadie nodded. "I figured as much. I could tell she'd taken a ring off when—" She stopped herself short, but it was too late to hide what had happened from an investigator like Virginia, who shook her head, emitting a low, throaty chuckle.

"Is that the real reason you had me look into her?" she asked. "You wanted to know who else she's knocking boots with?"

"No," Sadie replied, a little too defensively, but she knew she'd been seen. "I told you, it's for Astrid. She likely has a mole feeding information to the VCPD."

"Tell Ms. Dorefield to check the bussing staff first," Virginia offered. "They don't share tips with front of house, they're the most likely to flip first. But don't tell Astrid that, and make sure Ms. Dorefield doesn't either until she knows with full certainty that's what's going on."

"I won't," Sadie assured her, wondering when she was going to turn around and walk back down the stairs to the foyer. She waited, hoping that her silence would inspire that very result.

Virginia breathed out a quiet laugh, shoving her hands deep into the pockets of her coat. "A little advice, Ms. Sinclair? Don't be messing around with the wives of your opposing counsel. It tends to make cases stickier than they should be."

"I wasn't aware that Betty Coleman was married," Sadie admitted. "Or that she was married to a woman, or that it was—"

"Not Coleman, Ms. Sinclair. Ed Link."

All at once, the room seemed to spin around her, and she braced against the counter. "Ed Link?" she asked, hoping she had misheard, and knowing she hadn't.

Virginia arched one perfect eyebrow, a smirk tugging the corners of her lips. "Not what you wanted to hear, I'm guessing?"

"He said his wife—he didn't—she—"

"I don't think I've ever seen an attorney so shocked at the idea of someone lying," Virginia interrupted. "What a novelty."

Sadie stepped backward into her apartment, almost stumbling over her own two feet, her socks sliding against the polished hardwood planks. "It's not the lying," she finally managed to say. "It's the fact that Ed Link sent his wife to—to—"

Virginia snorted an indelicate laugh, covering her mouth with the back of her hand. "Ah," she said. "I see." She stepped over the threshold, holding the edge of the door in her hand. "You don't seem the type to invite in strangers or investigators, Ms. Sinclair, but as we've had plenty of business together before, I'm hoping you'll listen to my advice."

"What advice would that be?" Sadie asked, moving to the liquor cabinet above the sink. Whatever Virginia was about to say, it would go down easier with a good glass of red wine. "Lock the door," she said, still unnerved. "Can I offer you a drink?"

Virginia eyed the bottle in Sadie's hands and sucked her teeth. "Alright then." She kept her overcoat on but unbuttoned it, revealing a crisply ironed dark green shirt and suspenders underneath.

"Did you have court today?" Sadie asked, setting two large crystal glasses on the counter.

"I did," Virginia answered after a moment. "Had to testify in a divorce proceeding." She took the glass from Sadie and pressed it to her lips, taking a long sip before she continued. "Although, it's looking like I won't be able to dodge that subpoena any longer. I had hoped you'd be able to shut down this inquiry before it got that far."

I had wanted the same outcome, but things have become more complicated than I had originally anticipated." Sadie's jaw set firm, locked tight to prevent the escape of her honest opinions about Ms. Frost.

"Yeah," Virginia said, swirling the wine in the glass. "That's Astrid for you."

"Mm," Sadie demurred. She brushed a droplet of errant wine from the counter, frowning at the delicate stain it had created.

"Just try not to piss her off." Virginia took another swig and sank into the overstuffed chair across from the kitchen, knees spread wide and her forearms balanced there. "Now, do you want my advice, or not?" she pressed.

"I do," Sadie admitted cautiously, aware that despite her heroic antics, Virginia Vane was a mysterious, unreadable woman. "Is this about Ed Link or Astrid?"

Virginia tilted her head slightly, her moss-green eyes resting on Sadie's face. "Let's call it both," she offered. "First things first, Ed Link is after you, and you need to find out why. Is it because you slept with his wife?"

Sadie swallowed her wine wrong, and it burned in her throat. "I didn't—do that—until after he sent her after me," she answered.

"You're sure?"

"Yes, I'm sure."

Virginia nodded, taking a small notepad from her inside breast pocket and scribbling something at the back. "Why else then?" she pressed. "A case?"

"I would assume so." Sadie savored the rare vintage in her mouth, tasting every explosion of lightning that had fixed nitrogen into the soil, the cool breaths of coastal petrichor, and the rich, savory pleasure of crushing each grape skin before it passed into barrels. "Ed has never liked me anyway. He sees me as an irritation, and not much else."

"Whatever his issue is with you, it must be one hell of a grievance to send his wife to... well, you know. I suppose you were there for that." Virginia shook her head, running a finger around the rim of the wine glass. "Better it was Clementine Dorefield than that guy from the east side," she said with a sardonic laugh.

"The guy from the east side wouldn't have found much purchase," Sadie replied. "I figured it out soon enough that she was looking for information, but not why."

"Did she ask anything notable?" Virginia poised above her notepad once more, the pencil's point sharp and ready.

"There were some questions about where I came from," Sadie answered. "She didn't seem satisfied with my answers."

"And where are you from?"

Sadie poured more wine into her glass, watching it ebb and flow from the sides as it settled. "North."

"With answers like that, there's no wonder why she kept digging," Virginia said. "Where in the north?"

"Near the border," Sadie answered. "You won't have heard of it. Small town, remote, hard to get to." She swirled the wine in her mouth, savoring the dry pucker it drew from her cheeks. "There's nothing there for Ed Link to find, but I imagine he's hoping to look up my bar records to impeach my abilities as an attorney."

"Mm," Virginia muttered under her breath, scratching notes out onto the page. "Anything else?"

"No. Ed Link thinks I changed my name. I did, legally, but I'm a private person, Ms. Vane, so I had the file sealed." Sadie couldn't tell her any more than that, not without exposing a weakness, a gap in her illusionary armor that someone like Virginia Vane would immediately hone in on. "He's angry that I beat him in court. I got my hands on some confidential documents, and now he's trying to punish me for it any way he can." She sighed, her jaw clamping in response. "Including sending his wife after me."

"What did you do?" Virginia asked, pencil poised over paper. "Same as with my case, or different?"

"Different."

Virginia leaned forward in the chair, shifting her weight until she was resting both of her forearms on her knees again. "Different how?"

"I knew the State's Attorney had buried evidence. There was another suspect who left the country before he could be arrested, but they wanted to pin the entirety of the crime on my client, who was barely involved." Sadie sipped from her glass, relishing the gentle burn as the liquid slid down her throat. "A leak in the State's Attorney's office passed me a document. They sent it anonymously to my office."

"A leak?" Virginia was up out of the chair in half a second, pacing across the floor. "Ms. Sinclair, if the State's Attorney finds out that you—"

"I'm aware of the consequences, Ms. Vane," Sadie said, motioning for her to sit back down. "I am not naive in the ways of this city." She topped up Virginia's glass and set the bottle on the marble coffee table that separated the chair from the sofa, depositing herself on the latter. "I didn't submit the evidence, I had Ella show up in the middle of court with an envelope and merely allowed for Mr. Link's need to fill in the blanks."

"And he fell for that?" Virginia asked, giving a low whistle. "What a brainless ghoul. No wonder he's out for blood, he's angry that you made him look like a fool."

"I concur," Sadie agreed. "So what do I do now?"

"Hire Clementine, for starters. Astrid has a mole of her own and if she doesn't find them, then you can bet Astrid will burn this whole fucking city to the ground before she faces prison time. I can guarantee that neither of us wants that, given our prior dealings with her." Virginia drained her glass, setting it next to the bottle with the soft clink of lead crystal. "For the next thing, you need to make shadows-damned sure you keep your own ass covered. Captain Lindell—"

"I've inspected my records," Sadie interrupted. "Everything in my office or in storage has been examined." She rested the base of the wine glass on her knee, fingers wrapped around the clear stem. "Captain Lindell won't be a problem."

\#

\#

Chapter Thirteen

There was a strange paradox that lay between wanting to know someone's secrets, and dreading how laying those secrets bare may shatter comfortable illusions. Virginia Vane had carved out the truth, and Sadie sat in her plush chair long after the investigator had left her alone in her apartment. A glass of wine down, she was finally ready to face the cream-colored file with the red string closure, still sitting, waiting on her countertop to expose Clementine Dorefield's every weakness.

Sadie set the empty glass on the glass table in front of her, the metal accents showing off her own warped reflection. Edward Link's wife. She'd suspected that Clem was someone's wife, but certainly not his. Much to her chagrin, she'd managed to complicate her personal and work life in one fell swoop.

With a heavy, beleaguered sigh, she laid the file on her lap, the string staring up at her and begging her to unwrap it. The red string came loose in her hand as she unwound it from the button and slid the files out, a collection of affidavits used in previous court cases, photos of Clementine going about her work, mortgage deeds, performance reviews from her work, one arrest record for disturbing the peace, and two marriage licenses, one to Ed Link four years hence, and the other redacted.

Sadie held the paper to the light, squinting, willing the letters to reveal themselves from beneath the wide strip of black ink. There was nothing to make out, no clues, no nothing. The county clerk's office had been thorough for once, much to her ultimate and crushing disappointment. At least half the time, their redactions were incomplete, leaving hints of letters that could be deciphered, or not double redacting with ink atop ink to obscure relevant data, but whoever had control of Clementine's first marriage license had indeed done their job.

Sadie turned it over, examining the back, but finding nothing more than the Verdance county clerk's signature, the paper ten years old. She rifled through the rest of the folder, hoping for divorce documents, but finding none. Either Clem was twice married concurrently, or Virginia had missed something.

No.

"Dead," Sadie said aloud, nodding at the folder. "Clem's first spouse died."

There was no death certificate, of course. Aside from being a challenge even for investigators to get hold of, Sadie had asked her to vet Clem, not whomever she had been married to. Still, she felt guilty for knowing something so deep and secretive, something that Clem had not chosen to offer up to her in their conversations.

The shame of it singed under Sadie's skin hotter than the decent vintage wine, and she pushed the page aside as if it were made of iron and scalding to the touch.

The photos didn't tell any story that Sadie didn't already know. Clem went to work, ate lunch with friends, went home to Ed Link, of all people, and woke up and did it all over again. Sadie studied each picture, hunting for inconsistencies that weren't there. Whomever Clem really was, she was buried beneath layers of secrecy and untruths, unreachable to everyone, perhaps even to her husband.

Clem worked for several top law firms, which explained her presence at the gala as a welcomed and esteemed guest, and not just as Ed's plus-one. Virginia had included some recent court cases Clem had worked on, the evidence she'd provided, and some scribbled, barely-legible notes in the margins that were suppositions of how she obtained said evidence.

Bribed Barbara at the county clerk's office, one note said, with the name underlined twice in blotchy black ink. Sadie was aware of Barbara, the woman was a saint to anyone trying to nab paperwork under a tight deadline. Apparently, she was also partial to a tray of those nice chocolates from the place on Eighth Street and showed her appreciation with quick work, according to Clem's notes. The second page said something about an interrogation room at VCPD headquarters, but Sadie couldn't quite make out the name there. It didn't matter, there was no way for Sadie to waltz into the precinct without being swiftly tossed out. Defense attorneys were rarely welcome around cops, but impossibly alluring private investigators like Clem could sometimes convince them to cooperate.

The third note was crammed into the bottom left corner of the final page, with an arrow indicating which piece of evidence it was. Sadie squinted at it, daring herself to read the letters and stop staring at the paper through her fingers like it was about to spring up and attack her. The piece of evidence was what Sadie knew to be a drop gun, planted by two former members of the VCPD. She'd seen the case before, when it crossed her desk the first time. The clients had gone with another attorney uptown, and they lost. The previously missing murder weapon miraculously reappeared two weeks after arraignment, tucked halfway beneath a bush on the south side.

Pulling the page closer to her face, she tilted the page, trying to read what it said. Virginia Vane had totally illegible handwriting, and Sadie would have to ask that her new assistant be the one to write the reports from then on. Evidence locker, the note said. Clearly, Clem was more than cozy with VCPD. She must be doing them some favors to get access like that, to win their favor in rigging cases against the defendants.

It hadn't even been Sadie's case, but the injustice crisped at the nape of her neck, letting goosebumps spread across her arms. Realization flooded over her like a reticent tide, the waters murky and dangerous, the waves brutal and punishing. Astrid didn't just want Clem because she was a good investigator, she wanted the proximity to the VCPD. She wanted someone who would do whatever it took, someone who would plant a drop gun, or a felonious amount of Nether, or frame whoever the mole was, and make sure they were gone for good, whether they wound up in prison or dead.

Sadie sighed, burying her head in her hands. Not for the first time in her line of work, she wished she didn't know what she knew. There were days she yearned for the blissful ignorance of facts, of politics, of the gross and never-ending lies that whispered their way around the city, first from mouth to ear and then from ink to paper as the headlines screamed whatever the powers that were willed them to say.

Irrespective of what happened with Clem, someone was going to wind up paying the price for her creative investigations. Sadie rubbed her palms against her knees, willing the rough tweed fabric to jostle an answer loose from her mind. Astrid was expecting an investigator, there was no denying her that. If Sadie put up roadblocks, Astrid would make sure her business went to another law firm, one more willing to do the dirty work she needed to be done to keep her business afloat and her icebox stocked with the finest foods and beverages Verdance had to offer.

Drumming her fingers against the arm of the sofa, Sadie knew one thing—she was in for a string of long and interrupted nights.

\#

Bells chimed the next street over, signaling that she was about to be late for work. If she wasn't twenty minutes early, she was late, that's what her father had always said. Sadie brushed through her curls, fanning them out into large barrels, the better to cover her ears with. She tucked hair around each, being careful to not tangle in the delicate silver posts that lined the points on either side. She should have taken them out years ago, really, but it was one of the last vestiges of home that she still carried with her.

She hadn't wanted to leave, but when the safety and health of her people was at stake, there was hardly even a decision to consider. She had to leave, despite how painful the choice had been. That portal had welcomed her, even in her bitter ungratefulness.

Years had dragged on in Verdance, the gravity of the mortal plane dragging at her, reminding her it wasn't where she belonged, not really. Yet, back home, the same time would have passed in the blink of an eye. Back home, it hadn't even been a week since she'd left. Her name would still be at the forefront of courtiers' lips as they tried to impress the newly crowned king and queen.

Sadie breathed out an angry sigh, determined to ignore the pull of the past. The throne had been placed on her head within hours of her father's passing, and ripped away almost as quick. They'd never been close, but his absence still swirled like a void that was present in the marrow of every bone. His death, unexpected. Her duties to the realm, less so.

Specks of sparkling quartz gleamed in the morning's seasonal light, cool, crisp, and unbidden. She flattened her hands against it, absorbing the cold into her skin and willing it to clear her mind of all the distractions that had settled there over the past days and weeks. Her thoughts were too clouded, muddled, and murky, her usual precision dulled. Perhaps it was just that she was distracted. Perhaps it was the file on Clem, or the long, sleepless nights.

"Shailagh," she groaned aloud to herself, laying her forehead against the countertop, hoping that the frigid surface would ice out the thoughts there.

She'd been in Verdance five years and felt every single day, the weight of every sunset dragging at the human part of her. Every day, the iridescence in the mirror faded a little bit more. She tried so hard not to notice.

She pressed her hand against the counter and pushed herself back upright, buttoning her shirt over the ivory brassiere she'd already put on, the satin reflecting the gleam of the quartz. The deep sapphire cotton was a sharp contrast with Sadie's pale, porcelain skin, and tucked into charcoal grey tweed slacks, Sadie looked ready for anything that could come her way. She'd need the stature and the look, given Captain Lindell's hunger to ransack her office in search of materials to incriminate Astrid. Whatever the reason, the police captain had some kind of vendetta against Ms. Frost, that was clear enough. Sadie just wasn't keen on getting caught in the crossfire of VCPD power struggles.

Shuffling through her briefcase, she lined up the color-coded tabs on the right-hand side, alphabetizing them by the case name so that Ella wouldn't shriek with despair when she saw that her organization had all been for naught. Without Ella, there was no doubt she'd have a much more challenging time managing her client list.

Before Sadie could open the door, still chained after Ms. Vane's visit the previous evening, a knock sounded from the other side. The hinge whispered as she tugged her coat on over her shoulders, already concerned that whatever was on the other side would make her late.

"Ms. Dorefield," she said, hearing the exhaustion in her voice. "You're here, at my home."

Clem flashed a grin but folded her arms over her chest, pressing her breasts together to peek out from behind the deep v of her pea coat. "Good morning, Ms. Sinclair."

"What can I do for you?" Sadie asked, tilting her wrist to check the time. *Kelvaris*, she was already running behind. "More specifically, what couldn't wait until I was at the office?"

"I didn't feel like moving uptown today," Clem replied simply. "I thought this would be easier."

"I would prefer we discuss business in my office, not at my front door," Sadie challenged, willing Clem to get bored of whatever game she was playing. "This may shock you, but even attorneys value their privacy."

"Ooh, Ms. Sinclair, I'm afraid you forfeited that right and preference when you had me followed." Clem leaned her shoulder against the door frame, peering inside. "Nice digs. It looks like lawyers really do make bank in this city."

"The rent is extortionate," Sadie replied simply, unmoving. "What do you need, exactly?"

Clem threw off a husky laugh, leaning further into the door until her face was almost pressed between the gap. "The results of being vetted, obviously."

"Are you really that desperate for work?" Sadie asked, sliding the chain off the door and opening it wider, but still blocking Clem from entering. "I would have thought someone who works for some of the top law firms in Verdance would have more than enough work to be getting on with." She chewed on her tongue, biting back the snide commentary lined up in her mouth about Ed Link. Still, the words lingered, dancing across her vocal cords like shadowy temptation. "But if you're hard up, perhaps we can work something out."

"Still mad?" she asked, a playful smirk creeping at the edges of her lips. "Come on, Ms. Sinclair, I'll bet you've done much worse in order to win a case. Besides, it's not like we didn't have fun, right?"

"I don't recall that much fun, actually," Sadie replied airily, knowing it would wound Clem to hear it. "I'm very skilled at misrepresentation. A tool of the trade."

Clem faltered, just as Sadie had intended. She used the opportunity to lock the door, dropping her keys into her pocket. Clem followed her towards the stairs, chewing on her lip as though she was desperately searching for a reply that would let her save face. "I'm guessing that vetting turned over a few more stones than I'd anticipated," she said finally, trailing after Sadie on the stairs.

"Yes, you'd failed to mention that you're married to the man intent on having me disbarred," Sadie retorted. "But that is neither here nor there, Clem. I need to hand off these vetting reports to the client, and only then will you get an offer of employment, if she still wants to give one."

"First of all, he can't have you disbarred, your record is frustratingly unimpeachable, at least for now. I don't know how you've done it, but you've managed to charm or defend half the damned city. Admit it." Clem caught her by the wrist on the landing, gently reeling her back in. "Second, you just let me know that the employer is a she, which tells me that it's probably Astrid Frost, the siren who owns the Sphinx."

Sadie jerked her hand free, continuing down the second flight of stairs. "Who said she was a siren?"

"Please, everyone with half a lick of sense knows that," Clem protested. "How else would she be the top club in the city year after year by a country mile? People rave about that place as if they've seen a god or whatever is at the bottom of the Rift. Stars in their eyes, proclaiming their lifelong allegiance. People have lost their life savings there, Sadie."

"Mmhmm, I'm aware." Sadie reached for the exterior door, pushing out into the blustery cold day. "I don't see how any of this pertains to me, though."

"Are you saying it isn't Astrid Frost who's looking for an undercover private investigator?" Clem pressed, edging out in front of Sadie to stop her in her tracks, despite the icy drafts that toyed with the hem over her coat. "Secrecy, top-flight vetting, and that vetting being done by Virginia Vane? It has to be her. I'd ask if you know their scordid little history, but you defended Vane when that all went down four years ago."

"That case was dismissed," Sadie said, stepping around her. "Lack of evidence, no witnesses."

"Oh, come on now, Ms. Sinclair, you don't really believe that, do you?"

"I believe in the law, and the law had the charges dismissed." Sadie thrust her key into her car's lock and turned to face Clem head-on. "If you want to talk business, you come to my office. Don't surprise me at home. I imagine given your living arrangements, you wouldn't appreciate it if I returned the favor."

#

Chapter Fourteen

The courtroom that morning was dim, grey with the dull reality from outside, the cool-toned half-light almost too little to read the oaths chiseled into the marble behind the bench. Shadows cast themselves everywhere, pooling in the verges of the aisle and beneath the seats in the gallery.

Sadie relinquished her overcoat despite the frosty room, trying to avoid the draft that was so desperate to permeate deep beneath her skin. She subdued a natural shiver, willing herself to feel the warmth of the wool blazer tailored closely around her shoulders.

"All rise," the bailiff announced in a bored monotone. "Judge Haber presiding."

The judge entered, black robes flapping behind him as he sped to the bench. He was never one to hesitate, but his alacrity sparked a worry in Sadie's mind. He wouldn't be one to suffer foolishness, not that day.

"Morning," he barked gruffly, motioning for them all to sit down. "Ms. Coleman, did you manage to find your witness?"

Sadie held her breath, willing the answer to be no, they hadn't found the shift supervisor, and that the affidavit would stand.

"He's here," her client whispered, tugging at her sleeve and nodding to a man sitting four rows back in the gallery. His arms were folded over his chest, mouth set into a deep and uncompromising frown. In the back row, folded into her fur coat, was Astrid, pulling the lapels around herself as she scowled over at Sadie and her client.

Sadie bit back a Fae curse, not even having to wonder how they'd pulled in the supervisor. As far as she'd heard, he had moved out west to start a business with his cousin. Clearly, Third National Bank had deep enough pockets to not only locate him, but pay for his transport and lodging for the court appearance. "It's alright, we'll figure this out," she soothed, patting her client on the arm. Her internal beliefs were far less confident, and the realization of the inevitability of the judge's ruling sank heavier into her mind, allowing worry to nestle there and take insidious root.

"We did find Mr. Deerson, Your Honor," Betty chirped, flashing teeth at Sadie alongside a snide crinkle of her nose. "As it turns out, he wasn't so hard to track down."

The judge nodded, unfolding the files in front of himself and spreading the papers across the surface as he reminded himself of the details of the case. "Mr. Deerson, please approach the podium, so that you can be sworn in."

The shift manager lumbered to the front of the courtroom, favoring his right leg. Sadie winced, sensing that the injury was fresh. The train journey from out west wouldn't have been comfortable, and the stiffness in his gait was obvious.

"Do you swear to tell the truth and nothing but, so help you God?" the bailiff rambled off once the manager laid his hand on the worn cover of the old Bible.

"I do," Mr. Deerson said, mumbling to such an extent that the judge had to ask him to repeat himself.

"You have to speak up, sir," Judge Haber admonished, waving towards the stenographer. "The typist needs to be able to hear you for the court transcripts to be accurate."

"I do," the shift manager repeated, clearing his throat. "I swear to tell the truth."

Betty approached him, clipboard in her hand as she checked her notes. "Mr. Deerson, isn't it true that you made an error on your reports regarding Mr. Araday's performance in his duties at Third National Bank?"

"Objection," Sadie interrupted, standing from her desk. "Leading the witness, Your Honor."

Judge Haber considered his, scrutinizing both her and the witness. "Sustained," he said. "Ms. Coleman? Please rephrase."

Betty shifted her weight, looking over her clipboard again just long enough to shoot Sadie a dirty look so brimming with vitriol that it might have killed someone a bit more mortal. She nodded. "Your Honor," she demurred. "Mr. Deerson, could you tell us a little more about how performance evaluations are conducted at Third National Bank?"

"Yes, ma'am," he replied, coughing into his elbow and rubbing his bleary eyes. It was obvious that he didn't want to be there. He leaned forward, trying to make himself be heard by the stenographer. "We have bi-annual reviews for all employees, Mr. Araday included. We go through their reviews with them, and then they are filed away in the management office for reference if and when it comes time for a promotion or a raise."

Betty nodded, ticking off something on her clipboard. "Is there any chance one of these reviews could be misfiled?" she asked casually, smiling widely for the judge.

"It's unlikely, but not impossible," Mr. Deerson replied, words eking out through gritted teeth.

"So, in your estimation, there is a possibility that Mr. Araday's work review may have gotten swapped with another employee's?" Betty said, leading the witness but not enough for an objection, backing Sadie into the corner of the ring with nothing more than a toothless accusation of injustice.

"It could be possible, I suppose," the manager said, casting an apologetic look at Sadie's client. "But like I said, unlikely."

Betty produced a paper, brandishing it from the file like a flash of magic from the other realm, presented as the utmost in reality and truth. "This is another employee review that you conducted on the same day, Mr. Deerson," she said, sliding the page across Sadie's desk first, and then snatched it back to hand to the judge. "This review seems to indicate poor performance, chronic tardiness, and a disregard for safety and security protocols on-site. Do you recall going through this review with an employee?" she asked innocently.

"I do," the shift manager replied, shifting uncomfortably in his unrelentingly rigid wooden chair, the joints creaking with the effort. "Top brass encourages us to be harsh, in order to encourage a better work ethic."

"Who was this review for?" Betty held the clipboard close to her chest, tilting her head in encouragement.

Mr. Deerson swallowed hard, his Adam's apple bobbing as he did so. "I don't recall," he admitted, and even though Sadie had known it was coming, the sharp blade of the words still deflated what little she had left in her arsenal. He laid his hands atop the podium, smoothing fingers against wood, a nervous energy wrought by the pressure of Astrid's enforcers, no doubt. "The nights are always so late, and I'm always so tired. I worked two jobs to keep the lights on, Ms. Coleman," he explained. "It's rare I get more than a few hours of sleep a night."

"Thank you, Mr. Deerson," Betty said sweetly, turning to Sadie with an oily, self-satisfied smirk. "No more questions, Your Honor," she chirped.

"Ms. Sinclair?" Judge Haber prompted after a brief silence. "Do you have any questions for this witness?"

Sadie glanced at Astrid, who shook her head from side to side, a silent warning to leave things lie, or she'd pay the price for it later. Unfortunately, Sadie had never been particularly adept at self-preservation, especially when faced with an unwinnable crisis of truth. "Yes, Your Honor," she announced, standing up from the desk. She tapped the end of her fountain pen against her palm, creating a gentle, driving rhythm that steered her forward toward the podium and probably also toward insolvency.

"Mr. Deerson," she said, leaning against the podium, speaking clearly but softly to encourage him to be candid. "Did anyone offer you anything today for your testimony?"

"Objection!" Betty protested, almost rocketing out of the safety of her chair. "Your Honor, what Ms. Sinclair is suggesting is abhorrent and offensive, and I beg you to censure her for her conduct."

Judge Haber sighed, clearly already exhausted by the case and the situation altogether. "Sustained," he said, casting a furtive look towards Astrid.

"Of course, Your Honor," Sadie replied, her lungs burning with the sting of injustice. "Mr. Deerson, did anyone threaten you before your court appearance today?"

"Your Honor!" Betty shouted, almost knocking over the table as she stood.

"Ms. Sinclair, I am going to urge you to abandon this tactic," Judge Haber warned. "If you persist with trying to imply that Ms. Coleman or her client Third National Bank tampered with this witness, I will happily hold you in contempt. This is your final warning on the subject."

"Of course, Your Honor," Sadie said softly as Betty sank back into her liar's chair. At the back of the courtroom, Astrid stared, boring holes through Sadie a mile deep with its threat and its insistence. Sadie pressed her hands against the desk, willing herself to come up with a new strategy, but the walls were already closing in. She was between deep and deeper pockets, alongside the inherent injustice of the court system ratcheted up to the maximum volume. "Mr. Deerson," she began, steeling herself and her nerves. "What was your personal impression of Mr. Araday in the workplace on a day-to-day basis?" she asked. "Forget the performance reviews for a moment. On the whole, did you like or dislike when you saw Mr. Araday's name on the schedule?"

"I, uh…" he trailed off, glancing at Betty.

"You can answer without looking at the opposing counsel," Sadie interrupted, her voice syrupy with suggestion. "As far as I'm aware, Ms. Coleman isn't testifying." Catching the judge's steely stare, Sadie pivoted before anyone could object or hold her in contempt. "Mr. Deerson, in your time working for Third National Bank, were there ever cases of theft?"

"Yes?" he answered, once again looking to Betty to discern the correct answer. When she shrugged casually, he continued. "Yes, we had a few issues with theft over the years. A couple of hundred here, fifty bucks there. Never much more than that, it would raise too much of a red flag." He leaned forward, forearms braced against the knots in the wood patterning. "Top brass discovered that one of their own was dragging cash out of the tills and pocketing it whenever they visited a new branch." He shrugged. "It all got covered up, though."

Betty stood again, the wood legs of her chair scraping horribly against the tile. "Objection," she said coolly. "Relevance, Your Honor, what do other thefts at Mr. Araday's place of work have to do with his performance review?"

"Goes to character, Your Honor," Sadie interjected quickly. "If thefts were common at Third National Bank, and Mr. Araday did not participate, then it supports the view that his performance wasn't bad enough to be discharged over."

Judge Haber wobbled his head back and forth, eyes squinted as he considered the implications of both arguments. "Overruled, Ms. Coleman," he said. "Ms. Sinclair is correct and is allowed to redirect testimony or rebut where she sees fit." He sighed, waving a hand again. "Proceed, Ms. Sinclair."

Sadie nodded, bolstered by her miniature victory. "I'll continue then, Mr. Deerson, if that's alright." He shrugged, clearly uncomfortable with the turn of events, and Sadie herself felt the shifting sands of judicial appeasement beneath her polished shoes. "So you say there were a number of small thefts, all carried out by someone with a higher position than yours?"

"Yes, ma'am," he replied, eyes nervously flicking between Betty, Judge Haber, and Astrid. "But we didn't get any more details other than that. I don't think top brass even wanted us to know that much."

"Objection," Betty said again, leaning over the desk. "Hearsay."

"Mr. Deerson, how did you become aware of these thefts?" Sadie asked quickly, hoping he would answer before the judge gave his ruling. "Did you overhear this news, or was it something else?"

"No, ma'am," he answered. "Shift managers had to file our statements to corporate security. It was a third-party company, as they usually are when it comes to the transport of funds, but I'm sure they'd still have records of all that." He coughed again, a nervous tic from being under oath. "It wasn't hearsay."

"Overruled," the judge said.

"Your Honor, we would like a brief recess," Betty announced demurely, hands clasped in front of herself. "I feel we may be able to resist the temptation to waste the court's time today."

"Take five," the judge said, already disappearing back into his chambers.

Betty strode over to Sadie's table, one hand on her hip and the other still clutching the clipboard. "Alright, Sinclair, what do you want, hmm? A class action suit against Third National Bank? Well, I can tell you right now, there's no way you'll get enough previous employees to sign on. Class actions are public knowledge, and no one wants to be outed to the feds."

"I have no interest in a class action," Sadie said. "You are welcome to think that's untrue, but it's not. I just want to see justice done for Mr. Araday. His family depends on his income, and without it, things will get exponentially worse in relatively short order." Sadie sighed, pulling a sheet of paper from the folder, the bright green tab marked with an inked smiley face that Ella had drawn. "I have papers drawn up, in case you want to stop the inevitable dragging of top brass indiscretions into open court." She handed over the page, waiting for Betty to shred it into confetti, but she didn't. "We only want what's fair," Sadie continued. "This isn't an easy payout."

"Oh, isn't it?" Betty mocked, handing the paper to her client to sign. "Seems to me you just got the easiest pay of your life."

"It's pro-bono," Sadie responded, sliding the page to her client to sign, handing over a pen as well. "But thank you for your concern." She examined the paper, smiling at the result. After Betty skulked off back to her table, no doubt to lick her wounds and commiserate about dodgy, half-baked rumors, Sadie squeezed her client's arm. "This should last you about a year, long enough to find something else."

"Thank you, Ms. Sinclair," her client whispered, tears gathering in the corners of his eyes. "I never thought we'd make it happen."

\#

\#

Chapter Fifteen

Sadie wasn't halfway out of the courtroom when Astrid grabbed her by the wrist, pulling her into a nearby alcove shepherded on three sides by ivory marble pillars that rose to the high, vaulted ceilings of the foyer. "What do you think you're doing?" she hissed.

"Getting my client a settlement." Sadie freed her arm, rubbing where Astrid's fingertips had dug deep into the tendon. "And I did it in a way that Third National doesn't have to worry about a class action or creating a precedent for cases. These will be sealed, no one else will find out about the financiers' indiscretions." She straightened the lapels of her blazer, affixing the buttons one at a time. "I'm guessing it wasn't just small amounts they were taking, either," she said. "Financiers don't need to be pilfering a few hundred at a time, now do they?"

"I don't know what they get up to, just that they asked me to shut this down quietly," Astrid shot back, her voice barely above an enraged whisper. "I don't think you quite understand the weight of this, Ms. Sinclair, even after I warned you to leave this alone."

Sadie stepped around her, escaping from the trap of the corner. "I obtained a fair result for everyone, that sounds sufficient to retain your business and maintain your relationship with Third National Bank."

Astrid scowled, marring her usually picture-perfect face. "I don't like your *implications*, Ms. Sinclair," she said finally, indignation singeing the edges of her tone. "We have a symbiotic business relationship wherein I scratch their back, and they scratch mine, are we understood?"

"You can tell them the files will be sealed, Ms. Frost. You can also suggest to them that they maintain better records with regards to employee terminations." Sadie shifted her files from one hand to the other, straightening her posture back to her short stature, at least an inch smaller than Astrid, who herself was petite in size. "I know that things are changing in this country, but Third National Bank will have a class action from somewhere if they aren't careful with their records."

"You're lucky it turned out this way," Astrid snapped. "You don't want to know what they would have done if this had gotten out."

"Perhaps they could have your record expunged and your case thrown out, if they hold so much stature in this city," Sadie replied. "This case may be solved, but Captain Lindell and the rest of the VCPD are still watching you, Ms. Frost. You are person of interest number one in their search for distributors after Frankie Fiske went missing. There's blood in the water, and unfortunately for you, it's yours." Sadie breathed out a sigh, trying to regain her composure, inhaling a lungful of stagnant courthouse air, besmirched by months of wintery mold and the sweat of two dozen nervous defendants lining the benches of the hallway. "Clementine Dorefield is a good fit for your investigation," she said finally. "She's good, she's thorough, and most importantly, she's discreet."

Astrid raised one eyebrow, and then the other. "Do you think she'll find the mole?"

"I do."

"And you had her vetted?" Astrid pressed. "I don't want to be bringing in an accidental undercover agent of the VCPD or the feds for that matter."

Sadie's eyes followed a defendant, chained at the wrist and ankles, marching into a courtroom at the end of the corridor. "She's vetted."

"Who vetted her?"

"Virginia Vane." Sadie knew Astrid wouldn't stop asking until she said it, and she had higher priorities than playing obfuscation games. "It was thorough, as vetting goes."

"Vee?" Astrid asked, her voice smaller than it had been before. "Vee vetted this investigator for me?"

"She did, but wanted me to let you know she didn't want any trouble." Sadie squared her shoulders, her second attempt at regaining her stature. "Given the work she's done for you, I think it's probably for the best that you accept the vetting, hire Clementine Dorefield, and get this mole out of your club before they slip something more interesting to Captain Lindell."

"Trouble?" Astrid repeated, her face scrunching into a laugh. "Oh, Vee is so funny," she said, tacking a faux giggle to the end of her sentence. "She acts like she did time for that little charge."

"She almost did, Ms. Frost," Sadie said evenly. "It was by luck that they lost their material witness, and luck again that the charges were dropped before John Warren washed up on shore with irrefutable evidence that he had been present at the scene of the crime."

Astrid covered her mouth, laughing quietly. "I knew she'd never serve a day, and she didn't," she explained. "I'd never put Vee into any kind of real danger, and I think she knows that, deep down."

"I wouldn't count on that," Sadie argued, thinking of the late-night office call and the worry couched deep within Virginia's tone as she sat in the darkness. "Will you hire the investigator, or should I, to keep your paperwork in order?"

"You do it," Astrid asserted. "Easier to explain away a private investigator for you than it would be for me." She ran her fingers over the fur at her hood and cuffs, slow and methodical in her movements. "Tell Vee that what happened couldn't be helped."

Sadie's eyes narrowed, just for a moment as she contemplated her words. "You should probably tell her that yourself."

"She won't listen to me, Ms. Sinclair. She's all tangled up in some mess with a kid." Astrid shrugged lightly, the stray hairs from the fur collar glinting in the grey light from the large window on the other side of the hall. "I don't know what happened to her, but whatever it is, it's throwing her off her game. She should have been thanking me for leading her to Frankie, instead, she was shoving a gun in my bouncer's face." She frowned, her full lips set in a pout, the bright red lipstick a vibrant contrast to the demure navy skirt suit she was wearing beneath the coat. "Tell her to come home so we can talk."

"If I see her, I will. But for now, our business is concluded, Ms. Frost."

"Fine, fine," Astrid relented. "I always forget that not everyone wants to be useful, even when they're getting paid above market rate." She stole a glance at Sadie, a mischievous smirk playing on her lips. "While I'm aware that my attorney isn't interested in my personal life, I imagine you'll need to know what she'll say if she's no longer able to dodge the subpoena, right?"

"She assured me that she wouldn't say or do anything to implicate you in any crimes. Like I told you, she just doesn't want any problems." Sadie tucked the files under her arm, preparing herself for the journey back to the office. "Ms. Frost, I think that concludes our business for today, does it not?"

"Other attorneys would jump at the chance to secure my retainer," Astrid warned, though her voice was still light and airy. "Don't make me regret my choice, Ms. Sinclair."

\#

Sadie pored over Astrid's case files for the dozenth time, still willing herself to find a missing piece, or some technicality to have the whole thing thrown out, or at least a tolerable third option that didn't involve arguing in court. So long as she went prepared, she had a fair shot at proving that the VCPD had a vendetta against Astrid Frost and the Sphinx.

The problem was that what went on at Astrid's club was an open secret in Verdance. Visitors knew they could get a drink, a show, and a vial of Nether to make it all that much more exciting and all-encompassing. Sadie had never touched the stuff. She wasn't fully human, and as thus, tended to avoid human remedies. Medicine for a mortal might mean poison for her, hopefully a quick death, but more likely it would be drawn out, an exaggerated existence of decaying inside her own skin.

Cases piled up on the desk, one after another, an endless cacophony of Verdance's injustices. She'd spent five years picking through them one at a time, trying to right wrongs she hadn't been able to back home. Her strongly encouraged, self-imposed exile had been a surprising opportunity to atone for whatever sins she may have committed before she was old enough to understand the weight of their existence, before she understood the impact that one small motion could make The law was the only thing in the human realm that made sense to Sadie. Well, the law, and fresh blueberry muffins from the bakery.

She checked her watch, frowning at the silvery face. Too late for muffins, or too early, depending on the perspective. She shouldn't have skipped lunch.

The office door opened and shut, releasing an arctic gust that pooled around Sadie's ankles, drawing goosebumps to crawl across her shins.

"I'm back," Ella announced, tugging at the scarf tied tightly around her neck. "Shadows, it's cold out there. I'm so damned tired of winter." She unbuttoned her coat but left it on, hovering in the doorway to Sadie's office. "It's on," she said, her voice laced with both disappointment and fervor, a strange combination that only would have worked for her, and not for anyone else.

"They got her?" Sadie asked, standing up from her desk.

"Served about..." Ella trailed off, squinting at the clock hanging high on the wall behind her desk. "Thirty-five minutes ago."

"And she let them?" Sadie pressed.

Ella brushed a stray hair back behind her ear, barely concealing the impish grin spreading across her face. "I wouldn't say that. It was definitely more of a drop-and-run. They caught her at her office, some girl tried to intercept but she wasn't having it."

"A girl?" Sadie asked.

Ella nodded, unbuttoning her coat the rest of the way and revealing the cerulean dress beneath, the fabric gathered at the hip to flare outwards. "Yeah, a teenager, looked like."

Sadie stared, distracted by the lay of the wool and the line of stitching at the hem. "Did either of them see you?"

"It's possible," Ella admitted. "You know how Vane is, she sees damned near everything. She's like an oracle or something, always knows when you're there." She caught Sadie's eye and furrowed a brow. "Are you alright, Say?" she asked.

"Yes," Sadie replied, a little too quickly. "I was getting a little too caught up in these case files, looking for an error that I could use in court." She sat back in her leather-backed chair with the soft squeal of deflating upholstery, trying to think more about the case than Ella's sartorial choices. "When is the subpoena for?"

"Tomorrow at nine," Ella answered, wrinkling her nose with distaste. "I know. My guess is they're doing that to make sure Astrid doesn't get to her ahead of time."

Sadie nodded in agreement, drumming her fingers against the desk. "They'll have someone watching both Ms. Vane and Ms. Frost. At a guess, I would say it was Captain Lindell."

"No," Ella countered, shaking her head. "It's not her. I hung around Vane's office on Phoenix Avenue long enough to watch the squad units rotate in and out. Lindell's wasn't anywhere to be found." She crossed the office again, disappearing out of Sadie's line of sight long enough to hang her coat on the rack and adjust the creeping hem of her skirt. "I'm guessing the phones are also tapped."

"Undoubtedly," Sadie said. "It's going to be too difficult to grab her beforehand, and you just know Ed Link will be watching me like a hawk for any reason to have Judge Liesse hold me in contempt or to have me charged with witness tampering. I'll already be skating on thin ice, given I've represented both Virginia Vane and Astrid Frost in the past. Plus, that Third National Bank case that got all tangled up with witnesses and affidavits somehow managed to involve Astrid, too." She tapped a pen against the arm of her chair, a light, tinny rhythm emanating from each percussive hit. "It's unfortunate that Ms. Vane and Ms. Frost's histories are intertwined in several directions. It will make cross-examination a challenge."

Ella hopped up on Sadie's desk, one leg crossed over the other as she leaned back, picking up a file to read over it for the fifty-third time. "At least you know she won't intentionally incriminate Astrid," she offered.

"I don't want her to perjure herself, either," Sadie replied, the closeness of Ella's thigh sparking something dangerous in her mind. She turned around in her chair, choosing instead to stare at the blank wall behind her because that was far safer than the alternative. "I think she's smart enough to know better, it's not her first deposition, or even her second." Sadie ticked off her fingers one at a time as she counted through the occasions in her mind. "Fourth?"

she mused.

"A seasoned professional, then," Ella said, opening another file to flick through it. "She knows where her bread is buttered, and she also knows that she doesn't want to get tangled up in Astrid's business, right?" She set the folder aside, picking up another one. "I don't think you have anything to worry about."

Chapter Sixteen

"Ms. Vane, are you aware that you are under oath?" Ed Link demanded, doing his best to tower over Virginia at the podium, but she matched his energy, leaning forward until they were almost nose-to-nose.

"Yes, Mr. Link, as I have already stated no fewer than three times already, I am well aware that I am under oath." She smiled at him, but it was a threat built of teeth and promise. "And I will reiterate again, no, I never saw Nether being sold at the Sphinx."

Sadie tapped a pen against her palm, the rhythm silent but palpable within her. With little time to prepare Virginia Vane for the stand, she was having to rely on the investigator's experience in testifying. She was skilled, but so was Edward Link.

"This is ridiculous," Astrid hissed under her breath, bouncing her knee over crossed legs.

"Ms. Frost, shh," Sadie urged quietly.

Ed stalked from one side of the room to the other, his overly polished patent leather brogues clacking against the tiles, sharp and insistent. "Ms. Vane, you were observed at the Sphinx on numerous occasions across almost five years. You're telling me, this court, and the judge that you never saw Nether being sold at this club?"

"And I wasn't anywhere near the place for almost four of those years, Mr. Prosecutor," Virginia said evenly. She was unshakable, cool, and present in her forest green button-down and matching suspenders laid flat against her shoulders. "I would advise you to check those records again."

"Were you absent from the club due to your previous entanglements with law enforcement on the matter?" Ed pressed.

"Objection, Your Honor," Sadie interjected, rising to her feet. "Relevance."

"Overruled," the judge said evenly, making a note on a page in front of her. "Ms. Vane, please continue."

"I'm sure Your Honor is more than well apprised of why I'm here," Virginia said coolly, leaning back in her chair. "The prosecution is desperate to prove what's already been disproven. Perhaps it's a slow day for crime in Verdance?" she asked. "The charges against me were dropped, and the case dismissed with prejudice, Mr. Link. There was nothing there for the prosecution four years ago, and there certainly isn't anything now."

"That wasn't what I asked, ma'am," Ed retorted, tugging angrily at his ugly, over-starched tie. "I'm asking if your entanglements with Ms. Astrid Frost are why you were absent from the club for four years."

Virginia shifted in her seat, the first clue that she was uncomfortable with the line of questioning. "I don't think my personal life is relevant here."

"I think that a grand jury would disagree," he replied, his smile oily and snake-like. "In fact, I think Judge Liesse would also disagree." He gestured casually to the judge, shrugging his shoulders. "If Your Honor wishes for me to abandon this track, I will do so post-haste. If not, I'm afraid you'll have to answer, Ms. Vane."

The judge tilted her head, considering her options. "The witness can answer," she said finally.

"Yes, I would say that the trumped-up charges levied on me by the VCPD in a desperate and frankly, pathetic bid to drag Astrid Frost into court did have an impact on how often I wanted to be seen there. Despite my presence here this morning, I don't enjoy having to give testimony or become entangled in cases I have nothing to do with." Virginia braced her hands against the podium like she was about to stand, but didn't. "This may shock the court, but I have bills to pay, and when you're in the State's Attorney's line of sight on something they're obsessed with, it's difficult to get out from under it."

"Yet you've consulted on several VCPD cases," Ed pressed, sliding pages of forms across the judge's desk after showing them to Virginia. "From an

"Was there anything else?" Virginia prompted, looking coolly suave in her relaxed position on the stand. "Or am I free to go?"

"Hang on there, ma'am, just hold it a moment," Ed protested, holding up a hand as if it would keep her there. "I just have a few more questions for you, if that's alright."

Virginia shrugged easily, folding her hands atop the podium. "Be my guest, Mr. Link."

He stalked around the stand, doing his best to affirm his predation, his ability to hunt and kill but really, Ed Link was just an average man in an ill-fitting suit. He leaned over the podium again, trying to get Virginia to back down, but she didn't. She stared him down, motionless except for one raised eyebrow.

"Yes?" she prompted smoothly, remaining firmly in place. "Did you have more questions or not, Mr. Link?"

"Regardless of any consultancy you may or may not have had with the VCPD, there are still some concerns about your conduct in your line of work, Ms. Vane, questions that would bring your private investigation license into question." Ed smirked now, laying his palms flat against the wood. "Several accusations have surfaced regarding your refusal to report missing mythics to the police department, choosing to chase down leads yourself."

"Objection," Sadie said, but before she could continue, Virginia interrupted her.

"I wasn't aware that I was the one on trial," Virginia said coolly, turning to glance at the judge. "Your Honor, I realize this is just a preliminary hearing, but I do have to wonder why I'm being targeted here, especially when my work has nothing to do with the target of this case."

"Your Honor, her work has everything to do with the possibility that Astrid Frost is a distributor of Nether," Ed challenged. "She spent plenty of time in the Sphinx—"

"Four years ago," Virginia interjected. "As I've already stated, aside from the brief foray back to question her bouncers about a case of mine, I hadn't set foot in there, nor seen Astrid Frost, in four years."

"Objection," Sadie repeated. "Ms. Vane's personal life does not pertain to these proceedings, and neither does her work regarding other, unrelated cases."

The judge leaned back in her chair, fingers steepled atop the desk as she nodded, considering, taking her time to make a ruling on what was or wasn't admissible as evidence. "Mr. Link, do you have any more evidence that Ms. Vane would have knowledge of these alleged crimes of distribution that aren't either four years old or mired in police business?" she asked. "I can't imagine the State's Attorney would be thrilled to know you were dangerously close to dragging the department into another mess. Unless you can sway my opinion, I am inclined to sustain Ms. Sinclair's objection."

Sadie stayed standing, waiting for the judge's ruling. She knew Ed would anger the judge, given enough opportunity. He was too arrogant to resist the temptation to swagger all over the court.

"No, Your Honor," Ed replied through gritted teeth and a clamped jaw.

"Ms. Sinclair, your objection is sustained," the judge ruled. "Will you be cross-examining the witness today?"

"No, Your Honor," Sadie replied, not wanting to push their luck. Ed's missteps had cost him, and she didn't want to give him any opportunity to regain lost ground. "Thank you."

"Court is adjourned," the judge said, smacking the gavel lightly against the wood. "Ms. Vane, thank you for your time."

As the court room emptied, people filtering out into the hallway, Sadie waited at her desk as Virginia approached.

"Ms. Sinclair," Virginia said, and then glanced over at Astrid. "Ms. Frost."

"That went well," Sadie offered, directing her comment at Astrid even as her attentions were entirely fixed on Virginia. "But I'm not sure if it was enough. It depends on what the prosecution aims for next."

"They're going to go ahead," Virginia said abruptly. "You can tell that Judge Liesse thinks there's enough evidence to indict, and indict they shall. You know how it is here in Verdance."

"They'd better not," Astrid snarled, practically throwing herself out of the chair she had been sitting in. "How, after Vee took them out at the knees?"

"The judge wants to punish him, and insisted that the VCPD gets interviewed about their dealings with Astrid Frost." Virginia turned towards the door, refusing to make eye contact with Astrid. Whatever had happeed between them, there was no taking it back. "I'd be careful, if I were you, Ms. Sinclair. Prosecution rarely enjoys being on the back foot."

#

Chapter Seventeen

NEW FEDERAL LAW PASSED, the headlines read in blocky, four inch typeface. The words glared out from every newsstand she passed, their threatening imposition looming even before she'd made it back to the office.

Sadie knew before she saw her that Clem was tailing her. Shadows danced a little too closely after her, darting around corners, waiting for her to make a misstep that could lead to her own subpoena. Whatever Clem was playing at, Sadie was already on guard, watching over her shoulder for any shift in movement, for the flash of a camera lens, for Captain Lindell herself to pounce out of an alley with a warrant and a trumped-up charge at the ready. Clem was married to Ed Link, and Ed Link was no doubt in close contact with Lindell. She would be playing both sides of the fence, and Sadie cursed herself for not insisting on another investigator, vetted or not.

The State's Attorney's office was hand-in-hand with the police department, and everyone knew it, especially defense lawyers. Whatever one did, the other followed, covering each other's backs and destroying all evidence to the contrary. Sadie had seen it several times already, been shot down by judges, and seen innocents thrown into a cell for the mere crime of existing. The circumstances made her yearn for home, to return to the comfortable and the familiar. The pull was impossible to ignore.

Yet, she could never live with the consequences of returning.

Ducking into a small shop, Sadie made sure to linger just long enough to be irritating to Clem's watchful eye, before purchasing a fashion magazine she'd been flipping through. Human clothing was so intriguing, as though they all wanted to be seen and unseen at the same time. A paradoxical race, but one she'd grown rather fond of, despite the circumstances. She bought three different newspapers, despite the shared headlines about the new law.

Dirty bricks lined that part of the city, with tiny vortexes of minuscule trash blowing in circles. Sadie folded the papers and the magazine into her briefcase, flipping the brass latches closed. She spotted Clem half a block behind, trying to hide her face by turning back to the shop's front window, pretending to be interested in whatever fare they were selling. Radios, perhaps, or kitchen appliances. Sadie considered the option of confronting Clem, of chasing her back up the street, grabbing her by the coattails, and vowing to evade her, but she didn't. It was much more in keeping with her upbringing to toy with Clem, to pull her all over the city making moves that seemed meaningful, but fizzled into nothingness.

She took a bus uptown towards the Sphinx, only to double back on herself three blocks out and head east, wandering along the parade of shops with displays too pretty for a Verdance winter. Spring fashion still felt like an impossible dream, even though in two months the buds on the trees would return along with the songbirds, and the city would begin its descent into the humidity of summer. A chartreuse linen waistcoat caught her eye, paired with a charcoal skirt that flirted off the hip. A bold combination, but Sadie didn't dislike it.

The elevated train took her back towards the city center, and despite seeing Clem disembark at the same time, Sadie kept pace. The sound of salt crunching beneath her footsteps was a welcome companion in the quieter neighborhood, the roar of traffic dull at three streets' distance. She paused at a set of iron gates, sidling around them despite her multiple layers, walking around to the back of the public library. She crossed under the bare branches of a tall tree, their long, spindly fingers reaching out for a window on the second floor.

When she finally came to a rest, she waited to hear the crunch of untouched snow, hesitant, just around the corner. "I know you're there, Clementine," Sadie asserted.

Clem emerged, hands shoved into her pockets. "I should have known you'd be watching for me."

"And yet," Sadie murmured, tightening the tie of her coat around her waist to keep more of the chill out. "What do you want, Clem?"

"Just doing my job, you know how it is."

"Double agent?" Sadie asked, leaning against the brick facade of the building they were standing against, the public library. She'd chosen it for its inability to access privacy. The last thing she needed was a reasonable belief that she was colluding with investigators. "I told Astrid to hire you, but perhaps I shouldn't have if your methodology includes working for the State's Attorney."

"This is for Astrid," Clem answered. "I already tailed the bussing staff, there's one I need to follow up on, but the rest are clean as a whistle."

Sadie nodded, playing with a brooch she'd almost forgotten was still pinned to the lapel of her coat. "I wish I'd known your tailing and stakeout skills were so lackluster, I would have insisted she find someone else for the job."

"Maybe I wanted to be seen."

"Isn't it difficult to assemble a thorough vetting of me, if I know that you're following me?" Sadie asked evenly, ignoring the overly obvious come-on. "I just wasted three hours of your time."

"I knew you would be clean," Clem explained. "There's nothing on you, Ms. Sinclair, no matter who's been looking."

"Bit of a conflict of interest, isn't it?" Sadie questioned. "Your husband is the prosecutor, and you're using his access to vet defense attorneys?"

Clem moved closer, bracing a hand against the brick, a blond lock of hair falling prettily into her eyes. "Are you casting doubt on my professionalism, Ms. Sinclair?" she asked, punctuating her point with an uneasy laugh.

"I'm suggesting that you could very easily be feeding information to the State's Attorney as thanks for that access, and neither I nor Astrid Frost would be any the wiser for it." Sadie shifted, the wool of her coat dragging against the rough facing of the new brick, that patch brighter than the rest, newer, not as exposed to the realities of Verdance weather. "You haven't inspired a lot of confidence in your discretion, Clementine."

"Oh, I am plenty discreet," Clem argued, glancing back towards the street and watching several passers-by as they moved slowly against the biting winds. "What I choose to do in the privacy of my room doesn't ever pass my lips."

"I doubt that."

"I'm not helping the prosecution," Clem said again, tilting her head sightly. "You can trust me on that. I don't usually agree with his cases, you know. Why else would I spend so much of my time working for defense lawyers?"

"I don't know, you tell me," Sadie replied, still unsettled by the realization that Clem was married to Ed Link. "I'm sure that it pays better, for one thing. I imagine having the opportunity to have your cake and eat it too is rather tempting, isn't it? A comfortable salary from the defense firms you consult for, and pass information off to your husband for a happy home life. That would be sound ideal to most people, Clem. It would be a challenge to resist."

Clem ran the tip of her tongue over her lips, moistening them. She pressed them together and released with a small little pop, dragging her eyes back from the street to rest on Sadie. "I don't blame you for thinking that."

"Does Astrid know you're married to her prosecutor?"

"Yes."

Unseated by the answer, Sadie stumbled over nothing, having to catch herself on one of the black wrought-iron posts with a gloved hand. "Yes?" she asked.

"I know you think I'm deeply unethical, Sadie, but I have no desire to impeach my credibility to quite such an extent," Clem answered. "Of course she knows, I told her the moment she hired me. Astrid Frost sees my proximity to the case as a boon, not as a bust." Clem cleared her throat, a cloud of vapor emanating from her mouth and dissipating almost immediately into the afternoon sun. "She asked me to be thorough, and so I am. Besides, if I didn't tell her, you may well have."

"She's going to expect you to use that proximity," Sadie said. "I'm sure she thinks you'll be able to gain access to his trial strategy." She shook her head at the absurdity of the situation, feeling the distant rumble of a freight train that was about to crash into her life, upending everything she'd built. "I hope you're ready for this," she warned.

"I'm ready for anything," Clem replied evenly. "I thought you would have figured that out by now."

Grey sunlight filtered down through bare branches, pooling around them like ocean waves, waxing and waning with every breath of wind that swayed the leafless tree. "I don't think you understand what she's capable of."

Clem smiled, and for once, it wasn't a smirk, but something dangerously more familiar and casual. "I know my way around this city, Ms. Sinclair," she explained. "There's not much that would surprise me at this stage."

"I'm not so sure about that."

"Do you know how much Astrid donates to mythic youth charities?" Clem asked. "A significant chunk of what she rakes in every year. People aren't a binary of black or white, and neither is the law." She raked a hand through loose blond hair, the strands forming thick locks that caught the perfect breeze as they brushed against the collar of her coat. "Is Astrid Frost a bullish manipulator?" she mused, letting the words hang in the air for a moment. "Of course she is. But she's also why some of the kids in this city are still in school, still home with their families. You and I both know the feds are more than desperate to lose as many mythics in the system as they can before someone figures it all out."

"I didn't realize you had so many concerns about the education of mythic children," Sadie replied, tightening the tartan scarf around her neck.

"Even private investigators have a heart, Ms. Sinclair." She tugged a cigarette out of a rose gold case, engraved with orange blossoms. "Smoke?"

"Do you often smoke with the marks you're tailing?" Sadie asked, taking one and holding it between two fingers.

"Please, I've known for hours that you were playing me." Clem huffed an indignant laugh out through her nose, striking a match against the brick and lighting both of their cigarettes. "I was curious to see if you'd confront me, but you didn't."

"I decided that the more time of yours I could waste, the better," Sadie replied, maintaining the social poise of pretending to engage in the custom, but quietly despising the smell and the taste of ash.

Clem exhaled a delicate plume of smoke through rosy pursed lips, leaning against the building at her shoulder. "I wouldn't say it was wasted."

There was nothing to say to that, so Sadie didn't, choosing instead to stay silent, to try to forget that Clem had said it in the first place. Whatever she was after, Sadie wasn't interested in acquiescing. Clem couldn't be trusted, only in part due to her choice of employment, but moreso because her saccharine words were dangerously close to creeping past defenses Sadie had spent years building up.

"Astrid wants to see you before the grand jury." Clem was the first to break the silence, but her tone had shifted, becoming hardened at the edges, more businesslike and stark. "I told her that would be challenging, given the State's Attorney's ferocity for this case. They'll do whatever they can to undermine, to block, to make sure you can't come up with a viable trial strategy. They're trying to get you to use the phones." Clem exhaled the final breath of smoke, stubbing out the cigarette under the toe of her polished boot. "Don't."

"I know, Astrid is tapped," Sadie replied, extinguishing her own.

"You are also tapped," Clem whispered, leaning in close so that she was far too close to Sadie's ears, and she had to resist the urge to jerk away from the proximity. "And that's an example of something I shouldn't be telling you, given my apparent conflict of interest." She backed away, her face stony and serious, storm clouds reflected in her crystalline grey eyes. "People are rarely what they seem, Sadie Sinclair."

"So I'm learning," Sadie replied evenly. "Thank you."

"It's a two-hop warrant," Clem explained. "Nabs Astrid and anyone she talks to. They know you're avoiding the phones, so they're going to try anything to get you on them. There's a car out in front of your office."

"I know," Sadie assured her. "Two men, my receptionist confronted them."

Clem's lips pressed into a thin frown. "No, not them, Sadie. The other car they traveled with. Black, just like theirs, but dusty, like it was out on a farm or downstate somewhere. Make sure you keep your office locked. They won't break in, but if something is unsecured, you can bet they'll get their grubby mitts on everything. And shred any paperwork you're getting rid of, if you catch my drift."

"My casework is all above board." Sadie was filled with the sudden anxiety that it wasn't, despite days of careful searching. She was attentive in what she noted in client files, but the State's Attorney would do anything to get what they wanted—an easy arrest.

Clem nodded, satisfied with the answer. "Good. Don't let them get the drop on you, Sadie. They're out for blood this time, and they aren't going to let anything tank this case, especially not a one-horse firm like yours. They know Astrid is a quarter of your yearly billing, and in their eyes, that makes you an accomplice."

"I'm not—"

"It doesn't matter," Clem interrupted. "They want to put her away for distribution so they can continue to pretend that Nether isn't a problem in the city. It's good for polling numbers, you know? The mayor, the governor, the State's Attorney. All of them are just looking for ways to get reelected, and this would be a slam dunk."

"With Fiske missing—"

"He's dead." Clem lifted an eyebrow and then let it fall back into place, studying Sadie's reaction. "Didn't you know?"

"More or less."

"The Ruby Thorns are scattered, the Krakens are in the midst of some power struggle and have been for at least eighteen months. No one in the city can get their hands on Nether so now is the time for them to make it look like the VCPD and the State's Attorney are the ones who stopped it." Clem inhaled angrily, holding the air in her chest for a moment. "And when it inevitably shows up again, they'll all pretend that it's some brand new problem. They'll make up reasons to go after mythics, and we'll be on this same shadows-damned merry-go-round until we all die or the rift takes us all."

"Well, aren't you a beaming ray of sunshine and roses?" Sadie asked after a moment, unfortunately hearing the weariness in her voice. She'd only been in the human realm for five and a half years, but the politicking wasn't so different from home.

"It's winter in Verdance, Ms. Sinclair. There are no roses, nor sunshine to be had, I'm afraid."

Chapter Eighteen

Given both Clem's warning and the fact that Verdance was a place of increasing injustice, Sadie wasn't surprised when she returned to her office to find it swarming with members of the illustriously obtrusive Verdance City Police Department. Files were ransacked, strewn all over the floor like a refuse dump, and poor Ella stood flattened against the wall, worriedly pulling at her hands.

"Sadie!" she breathed, more a squeak than a voiced sound, pushing past two detectives to get to her. "Sadie, I'm sorry, they showed up right after you left for court and I couldn't get a hold of you."

"It'salright, I should have known they'd try this," Sadie soothed, patting her on the arm. "Captain Lindell," she called through to her office, knowing without a doubt that she was there. "I imagine you brought a warrant this time?"

The police captain appeared from Sadie's office, standing in the doorway and somehow taking up most of the space there with her broad shoulders and muscled frame. "Good afternoon, Ms. Sinclair, how nice of you to join us," she crooned in that whiskey-smoked voice. "I can't thank you enough for giving us the time to execute our warrant without interruption."

Sadie should have known that it wouldn't take long after that law passed before the State's Attorney's office would use it to strengthen their case. Clem. Of course. It was a ruse to keep her away, to give the VCPD plenty of time to go through her files unimpeded and unchallenged. Clem had baited her, and she'd taken it hook, line, and sinker. *Kelvaris*, how dare she?

"Of course, Captain," Sadie replied sweetly, despite the bitterness poisoning her tongue. "I'll always do whatever I can to help speed the carriage of justice."

Captain Lindell smirked, and it was mocking. "I'm sure," she replied, flipping open another folder. "Why is it that your files have all been recently examined?" she asked. "Not a speck of dust to be found in the entire cabinet. You wouldn't have been destroying evidence, Ms. Sinclair, now would you?"

"My records are thorough, and I have every legal right to rearrange my files," Sadie said casually. "As an attorney, it's my responsibility to keep my information organized."

"Kang!" Lindell barked, glaring at an officer standing near the door. "We're not done here yet. Tell your lovely wife she'll have to keep dinner in the oven for you, I don't care if it's pot roast." Her amber eyes slid back to Sadie, their warmth unsettling, given the occasion. "Ms. Sinclair, we have some questions about these files, specifically those involving Astrid Frost."

"Captain, if those were the only files you required, you could have waited for me to return from court. Furthermore, you could have asked my lovely and efficient receptionist. Given that she's shaking like a leaf, I can only assume you appeared shortly after I left and decided to pillage my filing cabinets." Sadie picked up a disassembled file from the desk, sliding papers back between the layers of cream-colored cardstock and repositioning one of Ella's note flags. "Can I assume you have located Ms. Frost's case file, or did you wish to continue?"

"We found it," Captain Lindell replied, stock-still and staring. "Unfortunately, it hasn't offered much context. There isn't much here." She advanced on Sadie, file held in hand as she waved the thin stack in the air to illustrate her point. "So as I said, we have a few questions."

"Does your warrant also include a subpoena?" Sadie asked. "I'm more than happy to testify as to the contents of those case files, Captain, but given my legal responsibilities as Ms. Frost's attorney, I can only do so if I am compelled by law."

The captain flipped through the file again, her mouth set into a frown as she considered her options. "I find it strange that you are practically begging to be subpoenaed," she said evenly, tucking the file under her uniformed arm.

The silver thread glinted, even in the warm glow of the incandescent lights overhead. "Why might that be?"

"As I said, Captain, I would never stand in the way of justice." Sadie strode to a filing cabinet against the wall, throwing open the drawer.

"Step away," Captain Lindell ordered, following her across the small office. "I can't have you tampering with evidence."

"Please, Captain," Sadie protested, waving her off casually despite the thudding pound of blood in her ears. "I merely wish to assist you in finding everything that's relevant." She tugged one file after another from the drawer, piling them up in her arms until she couldn't hold any more, and then handing the stack to Ella so that she could continue. "There are so many cases in here that may be relevant to your investigation. Here's one, in fact—a man who sued the city for discrimination. He won, but he was arrested for Nether possession six months later. At trial, we determined that the Nether had been planted on his person. That could be relevant, yes?"

"I don't think that—"

"Another one, Captain, a case where someone wanted to go after one of the bouncers at the Sphinx for unnecessary roughness. I represented Ms. Frost's interests, of course, and it did turn out that the complainant was very intoxicated thanks to Nether they purchased off-premises. Perhaps that's important, too?" Sadie handed that one over and opened the next file. "Here's one for you, I'm sure this one is important. A defendant charged with Nether distribution four years or so back, connected with Ms. Frost."

Captain Lindell snatched at that one, flipping open the file's cover and seeming to recoil from it. "I don't think this one is relevant, Ms. Sinclair. As I'm sure you heard in court this morning, these charges were dismissed."

"The State's Attorney seemed very keen to connect these charges to the current case, Captain," Sadie replied, folding her hands in front of her. "I thought that they may find that this case with Virginia Vane is of interest."

"It's not." The captain's tone had gone from cocky to abrasive and staunch, and she handed the file back to Sadie in seconds. "Our concerns are more recent, and more relevant to the case at hand."

"Relevant," Sadie echoed. "You'll have to help me on that, Captain. I am not able to discern what it is you're asking for unless you can provide me with specifics." She set the stack of files on Ella's desk, already dreading the unholy amount of work it would take to piece the office back together once they'd left. "I can't help but think that this warrant was unnecessarily broad, or improperly executed."

Captain Lindell's head snapped towards the door. "Kang, I swear to shadows, if I see you reach for that doorknob one more time, you'll be demoted back to beat cop by the time I make it back to the precinct." The officer held his hands up in surrender, backing away from the door, trying to hide the roll of his eyes but failing. The captain swiveled back to Sadie, and she folded her meaty arms over her chest, the silver badge on her bicep shining. "I think you may have to prepare for that subpoena, Ms. Sinclair, because these files aren't adding up. You and I both know that tampering with evidence is a class-four felony."

"Felony?" Sadie asked, allowing herself a light chuckle. "Tampering? Captain, I only just got here. How could I have tampered with evidence from outside the building?"

"I know that you must have shredded files, Ms. Sinclair. I am not a fool, nor am I interested in having the wool pulled over my eyes." She tossed a file onto the desk, disrupting the stack of the others. "I know that you're protecting Ms. Frost, and I'll make shadows-damned well sure that you get dragged in front of the same grand jury, stripped of your license to practice law, and hopefully that you'll never work in this city again."

Sadie couldn't quite discern why the captain's hostility had increased exponentially, but it was more than clear that she was edging towards danger. "I can assure you, I did not tamper with my files in any way," Sadie explained slowly, knowing it was dangerous to patronize Lindell. "As you well know, reorganization doesn't meet the threshold of a crime." She straightened the stack of files, lining up the edges one at a time, even as officers crashed around in her office, dragging drawers out of her desk. "I can appreciate your frustration in the matter, Captain, but I think you will find I have done nothing outside of the law. I am confident that the State's Attorney would agree."

"We'll see about that," Captain Lindell spat, stalking back into Sadie's office. "Take all of it," she barked. "Every last file, I don't care whose it is or when it was from. Get forensics on the line, we're going to need help in reexamining all evidence from these cases. I'm betting we find a very interesting pattern that points to Ms. Sinclair playing fast and loose with state and federal law."

"Not to be too much of a stickler for protocol, Captain, but your search warrant only covers files involving Ms. Frost," Sadie protested evenly, panic rising in her one capillary at a time because having her files raided and taken by the VCPD wouldn't be good for business. The idea of starting over again in another city was leaden within her, dragging her back to the terrestrial plane she'd found herself on in the first place.

Captain Lindell emerged from the office once again, arms stacked with files. "Yes, and as you very recently demonstrated, anything in here could be connected to Ms. Frost and her crimes of Nether distribution." She smiled, but the warmth didn't reach her eyes. It was hollow, an expression that promised nothing more than dismay and disappointment, along with the soul-sucking void that was a miscarriage of justice. "I hope this doesn't impede your work too much, Ms. Sinclair," she crooned. "I'd hate for another one of Verdance's worst to have to pay for their crimes."

Sadie bit her tongue and then the inside of her cheek, willing herself to remain silent. Provoking the VCPD any more than she already had would only end in more frustration. She watched as Lindell's crew of officers packed up her files, box by box, loading them into the backs of several squad units. "When will my files be returned?" she asked casually.

"When we're damned well finished with them," Lindell retorted. "But I wouldn't hold my breath if I were you." She leaned forward, taking the stack of files from Ella's desk, but left the one on Virginia Vane's case. "We don't need that one."

"Captain Lindell, I know that you think you're in the right here, but I can't help but think that this new policy of exempting lawyers from attorney-client privileges is a slippery slope." Sadie squared her shoulders with intent, trying to ignore the mounting fear pooling there.

"In cases of drug distribution," Lindell corrected. "Are you in favor of ruined lives, Ms. Sinclair? Because that's what Nether does to people, in case you hadn't noticed."

"Anyone can be accused of distribution, it's hardly—"

Lindell barked out a laugh, sharp and throaty. "Perhaps that's your experience, Ms. Sinclair, given the clientele you choose to work with, but it certainly isn't mine." She leaned over the desk, imposing, her square jaw angular in the greyish light from the window. "You've been aiding and abetting the scum of this city for far too long, and it's time defense attorneys learned to toe the line."

"Would you like to say that again, Captain?" Sadie asked evenly. "Perhaps we can get a few more witnesses testifying to the fact that you threatened me whilst carrying out a warrant on my premises." Ella pressed herself into the corner as Kang passed, letting him yank open her desk drawers one by one, the wood rattling with every new violent motion. Sadie breathed deep, willing the gesture to calm the angry seas within her. "I can't imagine that would look good to the board of a disciplinary hearing."

Lindell laughed again, this time lower, more of a growl than an expression of mirth. "I am the disciplinary board, Ms. Sinclair. I'm the deputy sheriff of this city, believe it or not. There isn't much you can do that would touch me." She straightened, squaring her shoulders and handing off a stack of files to a passing officer. "But regardless, I think you'll find that a threat didn't pass my lips. I was merely expressing my own political opinion on the judicial system, something I am more than within my rights to do, even on duty."

Boxes of files disappeared from the filing cabinets, were loaded into squad units, and carted away to the evidence locker, where Ed Link would no doubt take his sweet time going through them. It would ensure that she was powerless and indebted even more than she already was in the still-unfamiliar realm. Sadie let them go, hoping they wouldn't find anything that would endanger her clients. "Are you finished executing your warrant?" she asked, once the final box was hefted out the door. "May I return to my work?"

"Sure, sure, you can get back to work," Captain Lindell replied icily. "I imagine you have plenty to discuss with Ms. Frost, do you not?"

There was something about the weight in her words that gave Sadie pause, an underlying promise of destruction, or something else entirely more dangerous. It was almost a temptation. "As her attorney, we will need to discuss trial strategy, yes," Sadie said carefully. "I hope I can assume that there will be no interference on the matter?"

"Interference?" Captain Lindell asked, shaking her head. "Ms. Sinclair, it is every citizen's right to access legal counsel. I wouldn't dream of impeding one of the founding tenets of this country." She waved a hand to the rest of the officers, signaling them to exit through the front door. "You have a nice day now."

Chapter Nineteen

"*Kelvaris*," Sadie cursed under her breath, examining the aftermath of the raid. Papers were strewn all over the floor of her office, none of them related to the same case. It was as if a cyclone had picked up the entire building, shaken it around, and dropped it, scattering any semblance of order or organization. "How's it looking in there, Ella?"

"Like hell." Ella poked her head into Sadie's office, grimacing at the mess. "Well, you knew that would happen."

"I did. I had foolishly hoped it wouldn't, but the judge let the trial proceed." Sadie tapped the leg of her desk with the toe of her shoe, not brave enough to land a real kick and risk causing even more mess than they'd already encountered. "It's a good thing I left Astrid's trial strategy prep under the mats in my car," she ventured, flashing an impish grin.

"You didn't," Ella gasped, laughing alongside the surprise. "Sadie Sinclair, you are a force to be reckoned with."

Sadie turned back towards the wall, feeling the hot flush of embarrassment crawl up past her shirt collar and rest uneasily across her face. Judging by the blurry reflection in the glare of the frame holding her fake law degree, she was roughly the shade of an overripe beet. "I had a feeling they would wait until I had left."

"You were right."

"What happened?" Sadie asked, turning back when the redness in her cheeks had faded back to an acceptable level. "I hope they didn't treat you poorly."

Ella shook her head, but her eyebrows were still knitted into a frown. "Captain Lindell came through the front door, swaggering across the office, taking a real look around, you know?"

"Did she ask where I was?"

"No," Ella replied. "I guess she probably knew."

Sadie seethed under her breath, the frustration only seeding itself deeper into her marrow. "I would assume the same. And then what?"

"Said she had a warrant, Say. She showed me, it was notarized and signed off on by a judge."

"Which judge?" Sadie prompted.

"No one we know," Ella answered. "It's a new name on the roster, perhaps someone who is new to the bench." She perched herself at the edge of Sadie's desk again, taking the opportunity to lean forward and start to rearrange books on the shelves. "That could be useful, right?"

"It depends." Sadie let her swap books back and forth, creating a strange type of filing system that only made sense to Ella. "He could have been appointed by someone sympathetic with Senator Dean's aims."

"So much for neutrality in the judicial branch," Ella grumbled. "If Ms. Frost's case goes poorly, can you appeal?"

"Yes," Sadie answered. "If that happens, we can and will appeal." She sighed, running her hands along the desk's varnished wood, the chips in the finish catching against her fingertips. "We are living within a new normal, I'm afraid. One where judges and attorneys are at odds, rather than working towards the common goal of justice."

Ella tilted her head back until her face was illuminated with the yellowed glow of the overhead light. The window on the left didn't offer much, the weather outside still being dark, grey, and quintessentially Verdance. "That's such a romantic way to think about the law," she said softly. "Do you really believe that?"

"I do, Ella," Sadie admitted. "Every day I draw breath." She swept a crumpled piece of paper into the wastebasket. "Days like today make it a challenge, in truth."

"Are you going to discuss this trial strategy with Ms. Frost?" Ella asked, closing her eyes to the brightness of the bulb. "Will you go today, or leave it until tomorrow?" She opened an eye, leaning over to check the time from the clock on the wall. "It's getting late for today, business hours are almost over. That raid took longer than I thought it would."

"It would have taken longer if I hadn't come back when I did." Sadie was staring, but Ella didn't notice, so she chose not to care how obvious it was. "Did Clementine Dorefield show up in the office today? Or yesterday, even?"

"No, Say." Ella turned towards her, sitting up straight again. "Why?"

"I think she's trying to set me up," Sadie replied. "She's married to Ed Link, who'd have me disbarred, given half a chance." Her brow furrowed against her will, and she shook her head. "She still warned me about the phones—oh, Ella, I forgot to mention the phones." Sadie stood and crouched down near the wall, unplugging the cords.

"What on earth are you doing?" Ella demanded, jumping off the desk and reaching out to grab Sadie's arm. "How will clients contact us?"

Sadie yielded to allow Ella to pull her back, relishing the three seconds of contact that it had earned her. "We're definitely being tapped on all calls," she said. "Astrid's two-hop warrant put us on their radar. I called over there last week to arrange a meeting. I knew she was probably being monitored, but I was assured that it was only the business side. I was worried this would happen." She pulled out another cord, coiling it into a neat spiral as she went. "We can't risk trial strategies being overheard by the VCPD. You and I both know they'll quietly share everything they can with the State's Attorney's office."

Ella plugged the phone cable back into the wall, standing in front of it so that Sadie couldn't interfere. "Then we don't talk strategy on the phone," she explained. "In-person appointments only. I'll explain it as wanting to get them valuable face-to-face time with their attorney for no extra charge. I doubt anyone will argue with that."

"That is a fantastic idea," Sadie said, and meant it. "We will use that plan, then. In-person only." She stared out the window, craning her head to see the other side of the street. "Clem said there was a second car watching us. Have you seen one, all covered in dust and grime? Might have looked like a farm vehicle?"

"Not that I've seen," Ella answered, shaking her head. "And I've been watching, Say, ever since I tried to scare off that other one with the feds." She tugged at the hem of her skirt and adjusted the seam on her hose, glancing backward over her shoulder to be sure it was straight. "What do you want me to do if I do see a car like that? Approach them?"

"No," Sadie said quickly. "Just make a note of license plate number, any defining features if you see them, that sort of thing. I have a feeling that the next few weeks are going to be more intense than usual. That warrant, or raid, whatever they're calling it these days, was only the beginning. They're desperate to take down Astrid Frost, and right now, she's very vulnerable." She let go of the blinds, crossing into the office to check from there, too. Still, there was no dusty automobile to be found, and in fact, the only cars out front were familiar, those belonging to the bakery next door and her own. "I don't see it either. It's possible that Clem was lying. Trading false information to tempt me into handing over information on the trial strategy. I know she's playing both sides of this, I can feel it."

"It wouldn't be the first time an investigator has done that," Ella murmured, trailing behind her until she reached the reception desk, where she frowned staring at the overturned mess of the disturbed drawers. "I just got that reorganized, too," she griped. "You'd think the VCPD would have a little respect for a woman's work." She tossed a broken pencil into the wastebasket with a quiet thunk. "I guess not."

"Are you sure that you want to do this?" Sadie asked quietly. "The phone tap, the warrant, the mess, and the in-person appointments?" She surveyed the damage once again, grimacing at the mess. "This is going to be a great deal of work, and I don't know how bad this is going to get before the tide begins to turn."

Ella pushed a drawer back into the desk, replacing its contents one at a time. "I'm here for the long haul, Say. You think a few cops and some torn paperwork is enough to scare me off?" She offered Sadie a cautious smile that spread into a confident one. "They can't do this, and I can't wait for you to show them why."

\#

It was late, much later than she should have been at the office, but that was becoming somewhat more of a regularity. Sadie stretched her arms over her head and stared blearily at her watch, the dial glaring in the light drifting through the open blinds, the cold glow of the moon illuminating the face. Nearly three in the morning. The Sphinx would be closing, all of the patrons escorted out for the night and encouraged to return again on the next.

The streets were quiet for once, the empty void of sound almost unsettling in its peacefulness. Whatever the VCPD was planning, they surely wouldn't have waited all night to do so. It was much too late for public transit, so she would have to drive across town, surreptitious, doing her level best to not be intercepted or delayed. Captain Lindell would no doubt be waiting for Sadie to make even the slightest of slip-ups, any excuse to have her dragged into the station and charged with something nonsensical in order to expand the net of the warrant.

She didn't know what else they were hoping to find. They'd taken almost everything, leaving only a few files behind. The phones were tapped, her notes confiscated, and Ella was so shaken up when she left for home that she had asked Ray come to collect her. He'd showed up with a bouquet of flowers and a dinner invitation, wrapping Ella in the kind of tight embrace that Sadie had spent too many lonely nights imagining.

Shaking her head to clear the thought, Sadie finally stood from her desk, taking her keys from the hook just to the right of her office door. Ella had put it there shortly after the lease had been signed, the first show that the office was theirs to make their own.

The key slid easily into the lock, and the deadbolt clicked into place. She checked the front door and the side at least four times each before she slid into her car, rubbing her hands together before laying them on the steering wheel. She almost expected that the engine would stall, having fallen victim to some sort of targeted vandalism. Similarly, she was surprised when the car rolled forward onto the road without the telltale thunk of flat tires. Perhaps the police department was being more restrained in their movements.

The fact that nothing had gone wrong yet only increased the likelihood that something would, and soon.

Without traffic, the drive across the city was quick, every light green light as she went. Of course, the one time she required a little more time to organize her thoughts, the human realm saw fit to punish her with her punctuality. Near the bridge, blue and red lights flashed in the distance, and it was then that she knew that she hadn't even begun to understand the scope of what the VCPD was up to. She slowed, bringing the car to a stop when an officer flagged her down.

"Good evening, Officer," Sadie chirped, keeping both hands firmly on the wheel. "What's the trouble?"

The officer leaned in through her driver's side window, tutting softly. "I'm sorry, ma'am, you can't go this way. The bridge is closed tonight."

"Oh?" she prompted, keeping her stare straight ahead. "Why is that?"

"Ice," he replied airily, popping his chewing gum noisily. "Can't be helped. Salt trucks and plows can't get across until it melts at least a little, I'm afraid." He grinned, showing off one gold tooth on the lower left side of his jaw. "Can't be helped. You'd better turn around and head back."

"I think I can handle a little ice," Sadie said, doing her best to charm him with an overly polite and magnanimous tone. "Couldn't you please let me pass?"

He faltered, glancing around for his boss. "I don't think I can do that, ma'am," he said. "Strict orders. It's a safety concern, you see. Someone hits ice at the crest of the bridge, they'll slide all the way down the other side, maybe even crash into a pedestrian."

Sadie leaned through the window, surveying the bridge. "I don't see any pedestrians, Officer," she said evenly. "I promise I won't lose control."

"O'Malley!" a sergeant yelled from the base of the bridge. "The hell are you doing? Get rid of the dame and get back to your post. No crossings, the decision is final."

"Sorry," the officer said, his face contorted in apology. "I can't help you tonight. Maybe if he wasn't here, but—"

"Oh, please don't worry," Sadie said, putting the car into park. "I'll walk across."

O'Malley grabbed for her car door, holding it closed. "No crossings, ma'am, I'm sorry," he repeated. "There's nothing I can do."

"I hardly think that I would cause much trouble even if I fell," she protested. "Please, Officer O'Malley, can't you do me this one favor?" she pleaded, offering him a winning smile. "I have to get to the other side of town for work."

He glanced back at the sergeant, and then at the ice, and shook his head. "I'm sorry, ma'am, my sergeant made his orders very clear. I'm not to let anyone cross, not by car or by foot." He snorted to himself quietly, an audience for his own private joke. "Or boats, to be quite honest with you," he said.

Sadie released her grip on the steering wheel for just a second, enough to show him her devastating revelation that he wouldn't help her. "Thank you anyway," she relented. "I understand, Officer O'Malley. Not everyone has the power to make these decisions."

Briefly, she wished that she was the sort of person to drive through the blockade anyway, with no regard for the consequences. Regretfully, she put the car into reverse and headed back home to her cold, empty apartment.

Chapter Twenty

The next morning, the bridge was still closed, and traffic was backed up almost three-quarters of a mile. Sadie could see the tail lights from the office, a sea of red blinking lights, and the ever-present aura of quiet, simmering rage. Verdance residents had never been very good at exhibiting patience.

"I'll have to get across somehow," Sadie said, toying with the blinds. "I'll take the train."

Ella was still tidying after the previous day's raid, replacing drawers and their contents, reassembling stacks of boxes that had been cut open and ransacked. "They're going to have someone tailing you, Say," she warned. "I don't know if the train is the best idea."

"I'm running out of options, unfortunately. I need to get to the Sphinx to get Ms. Frost prepared for trial. They will put her on the stand for the grand jury." Sadie released the blinds letting them hang motionless against the glass. "She won't be able to meet here, even without the issue of the bridge being closed. Her car would attract too much attention, and it's not as though she'd ever consider taking public transport. They'll have agents posted outside the Sphinx as well." She sighed, half from frustration, and half from resignation. "We don't have much time. The clock is ticking, as they say."

Ella sat up straight in her chair, suddenly struck by an idea. "What if Ray drives you?" she asked.

"No."

"Just listen, Say!" she protested. "He's not on any of the rolls for the VCPD.

He has his work truck, you know, delivering papers and the like, and I know he'd be more than happy to do it."

Sadie restrained a grimace, seeing the inevitable crest over the horizon like a tidal wave of impending regrets. "The bridge is still closed, Ella. Ray driving isn't going to change that."

"They're letting work vehicles through!" Ella said, now more excited and pacing around the office, gesturing wildly. "Just sit in the back, no one will know the difference."

"And if they check the back?" Sadie asked. "What then? If Captain Lindell discovers that I hid myself in a work truck in order to prepare a defendant I've lost attorney-client privilege with, she'll be sure to confiscate my case strategy and find a reason to bar me from the case. Not to mention, that would implicate Ray as well."

Ella nodded, holding her chin in her hands as she walked back and forth over the parquet floors, each step a neat, clipped little percussive movement originating at the heels of her shoes. She snapped her thumb and forefinger, whirling around to face Sadie once more. "Get him to sign a retainer."

"Does he need legal representation?" Sadie asked, playing along with the game.

"Of course, Ms. Sinclair," Ella replied, laughing. "Get him to sign a retainer so that if you do get stopped, you're just there conferring with your client. We'll make up a story about how he wants to start a union, or unfair punitive action against him, or something. He has nothing to do with Nether distribution, so they can't pierce attorney-client privilege on the matter." She leaned back against the desk, her eyes sparkling with energy. "What do you think?"

"I think you're going to sail through paralegal school without a second thought and skip right to being a fully-fledged lawyer," Sadie said. "It's a brilliant plan, Ella."

"I'll call—" Ella held up a hand, interrupting herself. "I'll go meet him at his work, he should be getting off in about an hour. Early start, you know."

"You don't have to do this, you know," Sadie offered. "Involve him, your— boyfriend?" The word tasted like ash in her mouth. It was unfair, really, to dislike him so much, but some things couldn't be helped.

Ella nodded, grabbing her scarf and coat from the hooks near the door. "I shouldn't be long. You don't think they'll send a tail after me, do you?"

"They might," Sadie admitted. ' It's hard to know just how many police officers are assigned to this case, but it's safe to assume that most of them are. They are desperate to take Astrid down, and I'm getting the feeling that they would do anything in order to make that happen." She sighed again, this one more laden with the weight of life, and humanity, and all of it, and again wished that she could be back home, just for a short while, before everything had happened. Life had been okay there, until it wasn't. "Use the side door, and double back on yourself as much as possible. If you think that you're being followed, you likely are. Lead them across town if you can. Stop in a few shops, get coffee in a diner, or get a taxi. In fact, take two." She pulled a few bills out of her wallet and handed them over. "For incidentals. Buy yourself something on your way."

Ella waved her off, brow furrowed. "This is just part of my job, Say."

"Yes, and this is part of your pay." Sadie leaned forward, tucking the money into Ella's coat pocket. "Please don't argue."

"I'll be back as quick as I can," Ella said, rushing through the words in her excitement, almost stumbling over the last couple of words. "Shadows as my witness, we'll get you over to Astrid's today, I swear it."

As she disappeared through the back door, heading out into the Verdance cold, Sadie nearly bit through her lip to keep her composure.

It was a deftly and perfectly practiced habit.

\#

Ray grinned widely, throwing his arms wide at the back door. "Ms. Sinclair!" he shouted with enthusiasm. Ella laughed, shushing him with a light tap to his chest.

"Keep it down, Ray, this is a secret mission, remember?"

"Thank you for doing this, Ray," Sadie uttered, almost through gritted teeth. She offered him a smile, the same she would give irritating courtiers back home in Nos Prehn. "You are really helping me out."

Ray puffed out his chest comically, beaming. "Pleased to be of service, Ms.

Sinclair." With a broad, sweeping gesture, he indicated to his work truck the back doors open. "Your chariot awaits!"

Controlling her breaths to avoid a heavy, beleaguered sigh, Sadie slipped on her overcoat and scarf, knowing it would be frigid in the back of Ray's truck that early in the morning. "Ella, you should stay at the office, in case a client needs assistance. There are no meetings scheduled for this afternoon, but with the current circumstances, it's for the best one of us remains here."

"Of course," Ella replied, nodding. "And if Captain Lindell turns up?"

"If Captain Lindell returns, be sure to ask for the warrant." Sadie sighed, pressing fingers to her temples. "If Captain Lindell arrives here at the office, just do what she wants. There's nothing left for them to find here anyway. And tell her I'm out to lunch or in a meeting. Don't give any specifics. Be as vague as you can."

Ella nodded, taking notes as she bent over her desk, the darts of her bodice almost perfectly aligned, but not quite. "And if she presses for details?"

"Assert that you don't have them. I went to lunch with a client and you don't know where. You don't even have the slightest notion of which part of the city I'm in. Smile, be deferential, and don't provoke her. We already have the weight of the VCPD bearing down on us, we don't need more trouble." Sadie buttoned her coat and cinched the tie, tucking her scarf deep into the collar to keep out the drafts. "And thank you, again." She laid a hand on Ella's shoulder and squeezed gently, aware that Ray was watching her but he seemed more like a friendly stray dog than someone who would find that level of contact suspicious. The idea of two women together had probably never even crossed his mind.

It was almost endearing.

"Ready?" she prompted, stepping out into the daylight. "It's certainly cold," she said, doing her best to make polite conversation.

"Ah, Ms. Sinclair, you know Verdance," Ray said, comically strutting to the driver's side door of the truck. "If ya hate the weather, stick around five minutes, it'll change."

"Winter lasts for six months here," Sadie corrected, unable to resist the urge to argue with him, even as he doubled back to close the back doors for her.

"Just a second, ma'am, I'll prop open the inside window so you'll get a little heat."

"Thank you," she demurred as the latches snapped shut at the same time, the echo of the metal reverberating around the almost empty truck. There wasn't much inside other than an overturned wooden crate, two stacks of newspapers from three days prior, and one seat that folded down from the front divider. She sat, gripping the sides as the truck's engine roared into life, rumbling against her as he put the vehicle into gear.

Ray opened the internal window all the way, glancing at her from the corner of his eye. "I know that won't be much, but there's a blanket or two under that crate back there if you get too cold. I've got things on blast up here, but I know that's not usually very good." He chuckled to himself, shaking his head. "Hell, it's not usually even good enough for me, and I'm damned near sitting on top of it."

"I'm surprised it has heat at all, that's not common in work trucks," Sadie replied, doing her best to be courteous. "But thank you, I'm fine for right now."

"Newspaper wanted to be the first to get in on the new systems," he said breezily, pulling onto the main road in front of the office. "Too many delivery drivers quitting as soon as winter hit because we were all freezing our asses off that early in the morning. It's why I still have blankets back there, just in case the heating goes caput."

Sadie nodded. "A good plan of action," she replied finally, aware that the silence had gone on for too long. "And thank you again for your help."

"Aw, I'd do anything Ella asked me to do," he said, and there was a tenderness to his voice that burned in Sadie's ears. He turned onto the highway, aiming for the bridge to the other side of the city, towards the Sphinx and hopefully, the freedom to do her job without the prying eyes of the VCPD, the State's Attorney, or Ed Link. Or, for that matter, Ed's wife. Ray whistled half a tune before he stopped abruptly, turning to look at her when he reached a stop light. "Ms. Sinclair, can I ask you a question?"

"Of course," she replied, privately wishing that he wouldn't.

"Has Ella ever mentioned anything about getting married?"

An entire rockslide of resentment, regret, and a repugnant sense of self tumbled into Sadie all at once, nearly knocking her off her seat. "I'm sorry?" she asked, despite the fact that she'd heard him perfectly fine the first time he'd said it.

Ray blew out a sigh, easing the truck into gear again as they approached the base of the bridge. "I want to ask Ella to marry me," he said slowly. "I know she's it, forever and for always, and I just wondered if she ever mentioned anything about how she dreamed that would be for her. A proposal, you know."

"Six months seems soon," Sadie suggested, swallowing back the harsher critiques that lined her throat.

"Ah, I know," he said, leaning forward into the steering wheel. "But like they say, when you know, you know." He met her steely glare in the rearview mirror and his brow furrowed at the sight. "I know you two are close, so I thought she might have mentioned something." He adjusted his hands on the wheel, the cuffs of his uniform just a little too short for his tall, gangly stature. "I just want to do it right for her."

Sadie did her best to breathe normally, hoping that her discomfort wasn't as noticeable as it felt. "She hasn't said anything," she managed to eke out. "Not about proposals nor marriage, I'm afraid."

"What *did* she say?" Ray asked eagerly, that sad puppyish smile spreading across his face once again. "Anything you've got would be helpful. I'd rope the moon for her, Ms. Sinclair."

She didn't reply, for once unsure of what to say.

"So what was it?" he prompted, easing the truck onto the bridge, waving at a sergeant, though not the one from the night before.

Sadie pressed herself against the side of the truck, hoping an officer wouldn't see her through that tiny, heatless window. "She wants to go to school to become a paralegal."

"Oh," he said, relieved, blowing out a heavy sigh that almost rattled the truck. Perhaps it was the icy bridge, but the impact was the same. "Of course, she should do that."

"Perhaps you should wait on marriage until she's finished," Sadie suggested, her ulterior motive like sand in an hourglass, frittering itself away. "Just to be sure she doesn't get distracted from her goals."

Ray nodded thoughtfully, taking the truck across the patches of ice at the crest of the bridge. "I worry, Ms. Sinclair," he admitted. "What if someone else comes along and sweeps her off her feet?"

"I don't think you have to worry about that," Sadie offered, squeezing her eyes shut so she wouldn't have to face Ray or the officers outside the truck, placed there almost exclusively to keep her from doing her job. "Ella loves you."

The words tumbled out of her mouth, and their honesty was a specific and unfamiliar discomfort that Sadie had never had the misfortune of experiencing previously in her life. Unrequited love was like the sting of a rattlesnake bite, she imagined.

"We're through," Ray whispered, exiting the bridge. "On to our destination, Ms. Sinclair."

Chapter Twenty-One

Sadie slid into a booth in the Sphinx, strangely and overly lit during the day as cleaners worked around her, polishing every table to an almost mirror shine. She opened her briefcase, spread out the relevant files across the surface, and waited.

She waited ten, fifteen, and then twenty minutes, repressing sighs of quiet contempt as she waited for Astrid Frost.

"Drink?" the bartender called from across the empty venue, holding up two bottles, one of gin and the other whiskey.

"It's a little early for me," Sadie replied, but checked her watch and said, "Actually, why not." She pointed to the one on the left, the amber liquid enticing in the wake of Ray's admission.

He nodded, moving to prepare some artsy cocktail Sadie would never make at home. He assembled the ingredients, each bottle sparkling dully in the unatmospheric overhead lights, and rattled the shaker with enthusiasm before pouring and garnishing the results with a wide slice of an orange split over the edge of the glass. "There you have it," he said, sliding it across the table. "Ms. Frost will be with you shortly."

"I'm here now," Astrid corrected, swanning into the room like she owned the place, because she did. "Ms. Sinclair, it took entirely too long to call this meeting in the light of the grand jury going ahead." She frowned at the booth, but perched at the edge of the cushioned bench anyway, the silk of her pre-show robe pink and draped over the side of the forest green velvet of the upholstery.

"Yes, I do apologize, but the circumstances of your indictment have proved challenging," Sadie explained. "Between watching my office, blocking the bridge, and tapping your phone, my options were unfortunately rather limited." She sipped from the glass, surprised at how crisp the citrus notes were on her tongue. Of course, Astrid would have the best bartenders, the top-shelf liquor, and the freshest ingredients, she wouldn't settle for anything less.

"So am I in trouble?"

"It's common for a grand jury to indict," Sadie said, cautious in her tone and her wording, keenly aware that Astrid wouldn't hesitate to replace her, even that close to a potential trial. "However, we may have some leverage, if we can line up enough witnesses."

Astrid lit a cigarette at the end of the long, silver holder, resting it delicately between two fingers. "Employees?" she asked.

"That would be advantageous, if you are certain of their testimony."

"They won't sell me out," Astrid said, an air of both confidence and arrogance dancing at the edges of her words. "They know what's at stake."

Sadie shifted uncomfortably in the booth, despite the plush upholstery. "Are you sure they know what's at stake?" she prompted after a moment filled only with the quiet clinking of glassware behind the bar.

"Yes."

"Yes," Sadie echoed, nodding her head. "What would *you* say is at stake, Ms. Frost?"

"The Sphinx might just be a club to you, *mortal*, but to me, it's proof that the Rupture didn't have to change everything. Some things can remain the same, like music, a good cocktail, and crying in the bathroom because your beau dumped you for another girl." Astrid shrugged at her, aggressive and posturing, reasserting her dominance even though she didn't have to. "I'm not going to lose this place, Ms. Sinclair, I don't care how many people I have to throw to the wolves to make that happen." The cold sincerity in her voice, despite its florid, clear alto, shot through Sadie like icicles.

"I understand that, Ms. Frost."

"So tell me, what exactly is the plan? I have a show to prepare for, I don't have all day and night to sit here with you and your folders." Astrid cinched the belt at her waist tighter, highlighting the feminine curve of her waist. "What can they pin on me?"

"The prosecution is going for distribution, but we anticipated that." Sadie cast a glance towards the bar, watching as the bartender hung cocktail classes upside down by their bases, sliding each one along the wooden rail. "Ms. Frost, I need you to be honest with me. Are you in any way vulnerable here?"

"That depends what you mean by vulnerable," Astrid replied airily. "Clubs in Verdance are known for having certain contraband floating around. It's no different than any city, and the Sphinx isn't to blame for the ills of the local residents." She nodded at Sadie's cocktail glass, waving a hand dismissively. "All we sell here is what's legal. If they want to shut us down for selling booze, then they'd have to shut down every club, restaurant, and deli in the city."

"So you're not vulnerable in any way here at the Sphinx?" Sadie asked, dissatisfied with the vague answer she'd been given. It wouldn't be enough on the stand to convince a grand jury, nor would it be enough to convince the judge. "If you're honest with me, Ms. Frost, then I can do my best to protect you. Otherwise—"

"*No*," Astrid insisted. "Nothing illegal has ever been sold on this premises by any of my employees. If someone was slinging the stuff in the bathrooms, there's not much I can do about that." She caught her reflection in a mirror hanging on the wall behind Sadie, and rearranged a wave to better frame her face. "Please hear me, Ms. Sinclair. Nothing was ever *sold* by my employees or operatives."

Sadie leaned across the table, flipping a folder shut along the way. "I hear you, Ms. Frost, but the lack of an exchange of money may not be enough to get you off scot-free." She settled back into the booth, stacking the folders one at a time, checking Ella's color-coded tabs before she set them aside. "It is a good start, though."

"How can they still charge me with distribution if I wasn't selling it?" Astrid demanded. "I was assured that this was foolproof, that I wouldn't ever—"

"By who?" Sadie interrupted, already seeing the forest for the competition's trees. "Who told you that?"

Astrid coughed lightly, more to stall for time than because she needed to. "My previous representation," she answered.

"Who you parted ways with long before this new law took effect," Sadie pressed. "Correct?"

"I thought keeping on top of law and order was your job," Astrid shot back. "Isn't that what I pay you that nice, fat retainer for?"

"I can't keep tabs on what I don't know is happening, Ms. Frost." Sadie let a quick, silent hiss eke through her gritted teeth, laced with frustration that she hadn't known the score previously. She should have expected it, given Astrid's reputation. Perhaps she had. "Either way, we need to protect you from further charges being brought. Is there anyone you can think of who might have a grudge against you? Any witness that the prosecution could call as a witness?"

"Vee," Astrid replied almost instantly. "But she wouldn't." Behind her, the bartender wiped the surface clean, inspecting the marble for water marks before disappearing into the back room. "Would she?"

Sadie wanted to be sure, but couldn't—not given the strange, murky history the two of them shared. She hardly knew half of what had happened, and that was tempestuous enough. "Ms. Vane has indicated to me that no, she will not testify in a way that hurts you. She doesn't want any trouble." She sipped at her drink again, unsettled by the taste of alcohol early in the day. The Sphinx made them strong, and even halfway through her cocktail, her head was already beginning to swim with regret. "You should have told me about what was going on here, Ms. Frost. I could have better protected you, had I known."

"I'll tell you what you need to know, precisely when you need to know it," Astrid snapped. "It's entirely my prerogative to decide what details of my business and private life get divulged, is it not?"

"Yes, of course, but—"

"Ms. Sinclair, I hired you four years ago because my previous representation wasn't quite up to the task of getting Vee off the hook after that unfortunate mishap with the borrowed car and the Nether in the trunk. You proved yourself useful, proved yourself worthy, so I am asking you to please not slide back down into disuse." Astrid stood from the booth, twirling the robe tie lazily, the pink silk slipping through her fingers. "If they come to arrest me, you can consider yourself removed from my legal defense. Are we clear on that?"

"Crystal," Sadie replied. "But Ms. Frost, I think it's important that you hear me when I say—"

Someone pounded on the door of the club, the metal hinges rattling angrily with every blow. "Open up! We have a search warrant!"

"They're here," Sadie announced, pushing her drink to the side, wishing she hadn't acquiesced to it in the first place. "Ms. Frost, is there anything on the premises?" she whispered. When Astrid didn't reply, Sadie stood, standing at her shoulder just as the poor bartender opened the door and was nearly trampled by the veritable squadron of officers sent to raid an empty club. "Ms. Frost!"

"I, uh—I don't think so," Astrid stammered, now tugging at the tie, picking at the side seam with her perfectly shaped and pink-polished nails. "Probably not."

"Probably?" Sadie asked in a hushed tone, pushing past her only to come face-to-face with Captain Lindell, who had just entered the club. "Captain," Sadie said with a smile. "What an absolute delight to meet you again."

Lindell's eyes narrowed, arms folded over her chest. "I didn't expect to find you here, Ms. Sinclair," she said evenly.

"No, I expect not with that bridge blockade, and the officers you have watching my door, and the wiretaps." Sadie straightened, doing her best to match the police captain's posture and height, and coming up nearly a foot too short. "What is our plan, Captain Lindell? Are you going to have me arrested for meeting with my client?"

The captain waved over an officer, holding Sadie's stare the entire time. "Detective Kang, please search Ms. Sinclair for illegal substances and paraphernalia," she said, smirking. "And don't let her out of your sight. We can't trust that Ms. Frost's attorney won't steal away to destroy evidence."

"You won't find anything," Sadie said, holding her arms out straight so that the detective could turn out her pockets, revealing a silver money clip, three half-empty pens, six hair pins, a round, foldable mirror, and the keys to her apartment, car, and office. "Satisfied?" she asked, letting her arms rest back at her sides.

"Watch her," Captain Lindell repeated, just as another officer knocked into the newly arranged glassware, knocking several flutes to the ground with the disarming smash of hundreds of crystalline shards. "If you're going to tear the place apart, Officer, you could at least aim in the right direction. Do you see anything over there?"

The officer shook her head, standing stock-still in the center of the glass as it sparkled around her in the harsh overhead lighting. "No sign of Nether," she said.

"Keep looking." The captain stalked from one end of the club to the other, her long strides covering enough ground that she'd paced the length four times before she muttered something about the basement, disappearing around the corner.

Astrid stiffened, her hands flexing at her sides.

"Is there anything to worry about in the basement?" Sadie whispered. "Paraphernalia? Anything?"

"I don't think so."

"Now would be an excellent time to know for sure," Sadie pressed. "If they find even the slightest hint of Nether, they will take you out of here in cuffs and make sure half of the city reads about it in the newspaper. Lindell likely has journalists and photographers waiting outside." She straightened the hem of her jacket, already and preemptively preparing for a press release in the back of her mind. The law drew her focus, but public relations came as naturally to her as breathing—a clear consequence of her upbringing. "Detective Kang, was it?" Sadie asked. "Would it be alright if Ms. Frost changed into something more appropriate?"

"I'm afraid not," the detective said, the weight of apology in his voice. "Captain's orders, you see." He nodded towards the coat closet, open and already searched by one of the other officers. "But if she used the coat closet, you might get away with it before Lindell comes back up from the basement." He fussed with the knobs on his radio until a clearer speech pattern emerged from the speaker, a running commentary from the dispatcher. "I don't think anyone should have to suffer the indignity of being arrested only wearing their underthings.”

After the detective busied himself elsewhere, Sadie leaned in, whispering into Astrid's ear, even as she flinched from it. “We've got maybe five minutes until Captain Lindell comes back up here with evidence or something trumped up in order to arrest you. They wouldn't have come here in the broad light of day if they weren't planning to tip off the press before they arrested you. “

“There's a purple dress hanging off the back of my chair in my green room,” Astrid replied, not even moving her head, staring straight and standing stock-still. “It's appropriate for a mugshot if they insist on taking one.”

“They may.”

Astrid nodded, her jaw set firm. “And the matching shoes are under the table, left-hand corner.”

“I'll be back as soon as I can.” Sadie slipped away, past several officers exiting the dressing room, having just searched it. To her delight and surprise, neither of them was holding vials of Nether, though she wouldn't be the least bit surprised if someone planted one in the club for the VCPD to find. Ever since the Rupture, they'd been even more desperate to make sure that someone they deemed guilty wouldn't be able to escape a conviction.

Nodding at the officers, she slipped into the dressing room, taking the dress, the shoes, and the makeup case that was already folded beneath the lit mirror. Powdery dust laid across not just the case, but the counter too, laying claim to whatever was foolish enough to come into contact with it. Sadie brushed a smudge of the powder from her blazer, irritated when the gesture only made it worse, streaking across the fabric.

“Ms. Frost,” she said, thrusting the bundle into Astrid's hands when she returned. “We don't have much time.”

“I need you to zip me up,” Astrid hissed, dragging her into the coat closet and wedging the door closed with a forgotten cane, hanging off one of the rails. “This isn't good, Ms. Sinclair.”

“Tell your employees to let me represent them if any of them get arrested.” Sadie turned towards the wall, squeezing her eyes shut so that she definitely wouldn't see any more of Astrid than she should. “We'll form a collaborative defense. The strategy is good for both you and for them. If one of your employees hires another attorney, there's a chance they could go after you. In that case, the other attorney would use you, the club's owner, as a scapegoat."

"Zip."

Sadie opened one eye, and then the other when she'd convinced herself it was safe to do so. The metal snagged along the delicate silk, catching on threads that got in its way. "You should tell them immediately, it's the best way to guarantee they won't go with someone else. If the media gets hold of this, your employees will have every lawyer in the city offering them a retainer on contingency."

The door wrenched open, revealing a smug and smirking Captain Lindell, holding a small clear bag aloft. Inside was a singular vial of Nether, the purple fluid glowing, but only faintly. It was so old that it was practically inert. "Look what we found in the basement," she crowed, her whiskey-grit voice filled to the brim with self-satisfaction. "Ms. Frost, you are under arrest for the possession and distribution of a controlled substance."

Chapter Twenty-Two

Sadie watched as her top client was read her rights, cuffed, and guided into the back of a squad unit. It was a failure on her part, and a high-profile one, too. Astrid's arrest would be the headline of just about every newspaper in Verdance, with Sadie's name in black ink as the named attorney of record. Shame twisted within her like vines, the same way they had five years prior.

It was only one vial.

That's all it needed to be for the VCPD to arrest Astrid on the spot.

Press lined the street out front, flashbulbs near blinding. She'd expected it, but the sight was jarring nonetheless. Sadie steeled herself with one deep breath and a straightening of her cuffs, preparing herself for one of the toughest court battles she'd ever faced.

Sadie pulled the nearest member of staff aside by the starched sleeve, resting her other hand on his shoulder. "I need you to do something for me," she said quietly, aware that Captain Lindell was still roaming around the club, looking for more evidence. Planting it even, perhaps. "Tell the rest of your colleagues that Ms. Frost is paying for a defense attorney. It's likely that they will arrest a few more of you. Tell everyone to stay calm and to allow Ms. Frost to take care of them. Don't say anything to anyone if you're arrested until I get there."

He nodded, his eyes huge in disbelief. "I'm going to be arrested?"

"Perhaps, it depends." Sadie clapped her hand against the crisp white fabric covering his shoulder, offering him what she hoped was a reassuring smile. "Tell everyone you can, alright? I'll speak to everyone I can. Remember, don't say *anything.*"

"You can say whatever you like, actually," Captain Lindell corrected, swaggering across the parking lot to stand behind Sadie, her considerable height a definite advantage. "You don't have to listen to this attorney or any attorney. You don't have to hire anyone you don't want to, especially if it harms your case."

"Why, uh, would it harm my case?" the server asked, casting a wary glare towards one of the remaining squad units.

Lindell took off her cap, holding it beneath her arm. "Your employer may have nefarious aims, young man. She's known for throwing people loyal to her under the bus to save her own skin, isn't that right, Ms. Sinclair?"

"I think you should stop talking to my client," Sadie retorted. "Are you arresting him?"

"I don't know, I haven't decided yet." The captain loomed over both of them, making her position and her power known. "And he's not your client until he signs a retainer agreement."

"It's a verbal contract, Captain, perfectly admissible in this state," Sadie corrected. "Please feel free to check my work on the matter, but I think you'll find that I'm correct." Sadie holstered her files under her arm, the same positioning as the captain's service weapon. "Collaborative defenses are a significant benefit to the courts, they save time and are much more efficient than separate cases. I know that the VCPD's priority of late has been pursuing distributors of Nether." Sadie smiled at her, wide and toothy, not letting it reach her eyes. "But where were you when mythics were going missing by the dozen, thanks to Frankie Fiske?"

"I was the one who led the raid on that compound, thank you very much," Lindell shot back with a growl dancing at the back of her throat.

"After Virginia Vane wound up with a healer and took the brunt of it all, to my understanding." Sadie replied smoothly, her smiling sneer still perfectly in place. Growing up in a Fae court had been good for something, at least. "The VCPD didn't want to be involved, did they?"

"I was there, Ms. Sinclair."

"Yes, you were, that's true," Sadie relented. "Once private citizens did the hard work." She tilted her head as she handed a page to the server. "Fourth page, bottom, sign and date if you want my representation. You don't have to acquiesce to mine or Ms. Frost's offer, but I can guarantee that if you don't, the courts will assign you a public defender who may or may not be particularly interested in your freedom. Are we clear on the matter?"

"Yes ma'am," he said, taking the pen from her as well. "Very clear."

She stood straight, letting him sign the agreement against her back. She took the page, squinting at it. "Very well, Mr. Gonzales, you are now my client." She folded it in half, sliding it into a file. "Was there anything else you needed, Captain?"

"Astrid Frost doesn't run this town, you know," Captain Lindell hissed, the seethe of it oozing from each word as they crawled past her lips. "She would do well to learn her place, and maybe as her attorney, you can advise her of that."

"The Verdance City Police Department doesn't run this town either," Sadie replied evenly, producing another contract and pre-signing her name at the bottom, alongside the date. "Despite what you and the Sheriff might think, people still have a right to representation and a fair trial in this state." She leaned in close, her lips pulled tightly over her teeth. "Even if they are mythics."

Lindell jerked away, glaring. "That has nothing to do with it."

"Doesn't it, Captain?" Sadie asked, passing the contract to a passing member of the waitstaff. "Free legal representation if you are arrested," she said, and the young woman nodded, signing it right away with a black felt-tipped pen against the far wall, two tiny splodges of ink bleeding through the page. She handed it back and rushed off, no doubt desperate to avoid the press outside. "Mythics have been unfairly targeted in Verdance from the moment the Rupture happened."

"That may have been true at first, but it isn't any longer," Captain Lindell all but growled. "I've tried to make damned well sure of it."

"How interesting, then, that the State's Attorney is targeting the only mythic-run club in the city, isn't it?" Sadie continued with the contracts, passing them out to one staff member after another, each of them signing in turn without much hesitation. Many of them had likely seen the kind of damage an overworked, underpaid public defender could do. It wasn't a secret that in Verdance, in the entire nation, if you wanted a fair trial, and truly fair representation, you had to have the capital to do so.

"Are you going to make that your defense, then?" Lindell sneered. "Bigotry? Mythiphobia?"

Sadie nodded, rearranging the papers in her file, already knowing the workload to prepare all of them to give testimony would leave her without much sleep for the foreseeable future. "It seems obvious to me, Captain. You found one old, half-defunct vial of Nether in a basement, and you're arresting people? You and I both know that half of the clubs in this city have more than that stuffed under the sinks in the powder rooms."

"Astrid Frost has a history of distribution, and we can prove it." The police captain folded her arms over her chest again, muscles straining the navy blue fabric and the silver thread that seamed the pieces together. "The prosecution is already filing motions to keep Astrid from talking to her known associates."

"That doesn't apply to me, Captain," Sadie said, handing out another contract to a bouncer with a black eye. He looked it over, flipping through the contract with a raised eyebrow.

"Am I going to be arrested?" he asked, a waver of fear at the edge of his tone.

"Where did you get that black eye?" Lindell asked, unfolding her arms and moving closer, eye to eye with him.

"You don't have to answer that," Sadie said, offering him a pen. "Never talk to an officer without an attorney present. Especially not this one."

He shifted his weight from back to front, his shoulders squared like he was waiting for a fight. Maybe he was. "I have an attorney over on Eighth," he said. "Does that matter?"

"On retainer?"

Glancing warily at Captain Lindell, he bent to whisper in Sadie's ear. "Family law. Trying to get custody of my two kids. I can't let that get messed up, ma'am, I took this job because the hours let me take them to school and pick them up, and Ms. Frost pays well enough to keep a roof over our heads."

Sadie pointed at the empty signature line, trying to offer what she hoped was a reassuring smile. "Sign here. I will do my best to make sure this doesn't impact your other concerns." As he flourished an elegant signature, she stood on her toes to whisper back at him. "Ms. Frost always rewards loyalty above all else."

"I understand, ma'am." He handed it back with a curt nod for Sadie and a distrustful glare for Captain Lindell, rubbing at his bruised eye socket before he disappeared through the exterior door.

"You know you can't represent all of them if we get one to flip," Lindell said, straightening the silver badge on her bicep. "It can't be contentious, Ms. Sinclair."

"Are you studying for the bar exam, Captain?"

"I happen to know some very gifted attorneys and prosecutors."

Sadie smiled up at her, bending to pre-sign several more contracts against the table. Thank goodness for Ella, who'd sent her with plenty. "Yes, and it's a pleasure to make your acquaintance. Thank you for the compliment."

"I was referring to Ed Link."

"I am well aware, Captain Lindell." One page after another, signed and passed along to Astrid's employees. "If you see him, tell Mr. Link that I look forward to facing him in court."

Lindell's brow furrowed, confusion sinking deep into the fine lines at the corners of her eyes. "If you're trying to undermine me, Ms. Sinclair, I'm afraid you have a bigger job ahead of you. I am not so easily cowed as other officers. I'm the deputy sheriff, and I didn't get that position by bending the knee to singleton lawyers in tiny offices, or by letting obvious criminal enterprise continue unchecked just because the head of it happens to be a mythic, or a paragon of the community, or—"

"Or an officer?" Sadie supplied. She'd heard plenty about how the VCPD was run, and not just from Virginia Vane.

"Do you have something you want to say, Ms. Sinclair?" Lindell asked sweetly, the sardonic laugh caught in her throat like ash and honey. "Because if so, I suggest you spit it out. I have no interest in verbally fencing with you, especially when I'm well aware that you're stalling. You're trying to keep me from questioning my star witness."

"You can question her if you wish, Captain. I doubt Ms. Frost will offer up anything you could find useful. She knows better than to speak to detectives without me present." Sadie shuffled the papers, quickly alphabetizing them as she worked. "And she's dealt with enough to know that you don't exactly have her best interests at heart. How often have you been staking this place out over the past few months?"

"That's classified."

"Of course it is, Captain," Sadie allowed, snapping the file shut. The rest of the club had emptied, so she left a stack of business cards behind the bar with a note scribbled on a napkin. "I wouldn't expect anything else of you, or the VCPD, for that matter. The truth of the matter is that your entire department has been engaged in a long-form harassment campaign against Ms. Frost due to her status as a mythic. I'm sure the fact that the police commissioner was seen here under the influence has nothing to do with Ms. Frost's indictment."

"The police commissioner—"

"Is a good man, I'm sure," Sadie interjected. "But that doesn't change the facts of this case."

"Astrid Frost has been a thorn in my side since the day I arrived in Verdance," Lindell all but spat, towering over Sadie, hand resting on the service revolver at her hip. "She's been allowed to run rampant, to distribute huge amounts of Nether unchecked, and to pin whatever she wanted on innocent bystanders, who are the ones who actually pay the price for her crimes."

"Like Virginia Vane?" Sadie asked, an eyebrow raised.

"Sure," Lindell admitted. "Among others."

The overhead lights flickered, just once. Someone must have been checking the fuse box in the basement, no doubt looking for more Nether but not finding it. "Captain Lindell, you and I aren't going to see eye-to-eye on this or much else, so I would guess that it's prudent for us to stay out of each other's way." Sadie slid the rest of her files into her leather briefcase, flicking the brass latches closed with a sharp flick. "It was nice seeing you again, Captain."

"I'm not letting you out of my sight, Ms. Sinclair," Lindell said in a low, threatening voice. "It's probably for the best that you get very used to me looking over your shoulder. You make one mistake, and I'll find it. If you so much as even think about doing something illegal or unethical, I'll know, and I'll make shadows-damned sure that you pay the price for it, whether that looks like contempt of court or your license being revoked."

"Language, please," Sadie chastised, tutting softly. "I'd hate to offend the delicate sensibilities of the VCPD, Captain."

"We're not so fragile as you might think."

"And you should know that if you watch me, I'll make sure I'm watching right back." Sadie gave her one last smile, hand pressed against the door to the club. "And you and I both know that there's plenty of nothing to see within the walls of VCPD headquarters."

\#

Chapter Twenty-Three

Astrid Frost did nott suit a jail cell Hair unkempt and mussed, her dress wrinkled at the back and a run in her hose, she looked more like an angry, feral cat than a beautiful, jazz-singing siren. "It took you long enough," she spat, sidling between the bars.

"The judge was not thrilled about granting you bail," Sadie explained. "The prosecutor wanted to push that you were a flight risk. He didn't want you to be able to get out at all. He wanted to have you transferred to county until the trial."

"And when is that?" Astrid snapped. "Or did you drop the ball on that, too?" She caught her reflection in a window, pausing to rearrange a wave against her face and smooth the creases in the purple fabric. "I'm sorry, this has all just been too much for me, Ms. Sinclair."

Sadie nodded, trailing behind her. "I understand completely, Ms. Frost." She followed her past the intake booth where one of her bartenders was being given a mugshot and stifled a grimace, already feeling the weight of several sleepless nights. "I was able to argue that your club is an anchor for you, and that you would never abandon it or leave it in anyone else's hands."

"I know what I said before, but I would if it kept me out of prison," Astrid grumbled.

"Shh."

"I put my heart and soul into that place, and I will be shadows-damned if I let it go to the dogs or the crews," she said, louder this time.

Sadie nodded. "Good. Better."

"It's a travesty how the VCPD treats mythics in this city!" Astrid continued, her crystalline voice carrying easily throughout the corridors. "I've done nothing wrong, and not only are they targeting me, but my employees as well! It's a disgrace! An outrage!"

"I think that is sufficient," Sadie soothed. She waved at reception as they passed, pointing out towards her car. "We need to go over trial preparations," she explained. "The VCPD gave up on blocking the bridge once you were arrested, I suppose because they got what they were looking for." She unlocked the doors, holding open the passenger side for Astrid. "I secured retainer agreements from eighty percent of your staff, and from what I understand, the other twenty percent are forthcoming. That is a very positive sign, Ms. Frost."

"I try to treat my people well," Astrid explained. "I may not do everything perfectly, but paying people and supporting them makes them far more loyal than threats do. In this shadows-damned city where crews are forever trying to poach my bouncers and my bartenders, I've found it works rather well." She climbed in, sliding across the leather. "And in times of trouble, it's loyalty that wins out."

A squad unit pulled into the lot, the bouncer with the black eye hanging his head low in the back seat. He was mouthing something at Sadie as the car came to a stop, but she'd never been particularly adept at lip-reading.

"Oh no," Astrid said, immediately releasing the buckle. "They got George. Ms. Sinclair, he's one of my best, and he has a case in family court."

"Yes," Sadie assuaged, already striding across the parking lot. "Two children, family court. He'll never get his children back if he has a record implying drug distribution." She approached the squad unit, grinning through the windshield at Detective Kang. "Good evening, sir," she said, leaning against his door. "May I ask what you're doing with my client?"

"Charged with possession," Kang replied gruffly. "Procedure."

"Procedure, yes," Sadie said, nodding. "Possession of what?"

"Controlled substances."

"Do you have proof?"

Kang rolled his eyes, but gave a worried glance into the back seat. "Proof enough," he answered. "Get away from my door before I call backup."

Lifting her hands in surrender, Sadie backed away, showing her palms in deference to the man with not one, but two service revolvers holstered at his hips. "You cannot arrest citizens without cause," she warned. "I'll have your badge if you're not careful, Detective."

"Ms. Sinclair, if you don't get the hell out of this parking lot, I'll have *you* arrested," Captain Lindell said from the back steps of the building. "Detective Kang, please escort your charge in for processing, and make it snappy, please, we have three more on their way."

"I have a right to be here," Sadie retorted. "My clients have a right to their representation."

"Not when their representation is being escorted from the premises for disruption." Lindell smiled, leaning easily against the iron hand railing. "Don't test me, Ms. Sinclair, I'm not in the mood for games."

Sadie left Astrid shivering in the car, approaching the steps with all five foot one of her height, injustice starting to crisp the underside of her skin. "This is unconscionable, Captain," she said, her clear voice echoing across the courtyard. "You heard what my client said at the club, and you're going to use him and his situation for your own gain."

"I don't know what you're talking about, first of all, and second, even if I was doing something below-board, it's nothing less than the rest of the defense attorneys in this city do." Lindell cuffed her sleeves, showing off the olive-toned skin and taut forearms beneath the thick wool. "Maybe it's time the VCPD played the same games."

"The VCPD is well-versed in these tactics," Sadie said. "You're targeting mythics because you know that the press will be sympathetic. It's an outrage, Captain, and I'm not going to stand for it."

"You have no idea what this job entails."

"I know that you are threatening my client with an arrest record, only because you are bound and determined to see Astrid Frost behind bars."

Lindell smirked again. "It's where she belongs. She's a known Nether distributor, and we have proof."

"How can she be a known distributor with one vial of Nether?" Sadie asked, shaking her head. "It's preposterous, and this is nothing more than a grudge from your department." Her eyes narrowed, and she leaned in closer, head tilted. "Or perhaps the grudge is more personal than at the department level?"

"Nonsense." Lindell waved her off, moving to go back into the precinct. "All any of us are doing is trying to keep this garbage off the streets, although I realize that may be a foreign concept to a defense attorney."

"Release my client, Captain Lindell." Sadie allowed herself to have an edge of pleading, of earnest desperation. "Please, you know he has nothing to do with this."

"Unfortunately, for him, he has everything to do with this." The captain waved at the squad unit, motioning for them to climb the steps into the building. "This is a foregone conclusion, Ms. Sinclair. To back away now would be unethical."

#

Sadie breathed out a streak of Fae curses, pulling at the cuffs of her sleeves. Three witnesses and co-defendants had been scooped up from the Sphinx in the raid, each of them being held without bail thanks to Ed Link convincing Judge Liesse that they could be influenced by their employer, Astrid.

"I'm guessing it went well, then?" Ella asked, sliding a mug of steaming black coffee across the desk. "Ray said you got to the Sphinx okay."

"Yes," Sadie admitted, realizing the frustrating weight of the entire situation. "Tell him I said thank you. If I hadn't been there, things would be immeasurably worse."

"Ms. Frost has called fourteen times, Say. I don't know what else to tell her when she calls..." Ella trailed off, fishing for an answer to the question she didn't want to ask.

"I'll return her call the moment I've had a chance to catch my breath. I've been in bail hearings all morning." Sadie buried her face in her hands, digging her short nails into her scalp. "One of our clients might lose his children over this, and he didn't even have anything to do with it." She shuffled through papers once more, hoping that an answer might present itself. "The VCPD—Captain Lindell, specifically, and Ed Link at the State's Attorney's office—will use his case in family court to get him to testify against Astrid, I'm sure of it."

"That's pretty low." Ella perched on the corner of Sadie's desk, crossing one leg over the other, the wool of her skirt draped prettily over her thigh and knee. "What are we going to do?"

Sadie couldn't help but smile at the inclusion of *we* in Ella's comment, but swallowed it back into her mouth almost immediately. "We need to get our client out of there. We need to get him released, first and foremost, and then we need to have these charges dropped. Otherwise..."

"Otherwise, there's a chance he sides with the prosecution, and the whole collaborative defense collapses," Ella supplied, nodding thoughtfully. "What can Ms. Frost do?"

"She's likely in a state of panic. There isn't much she can do beyond wait, but that unfortunately isn't going to keep her from thinking that I should be able to fix everything instantaneously." Sadie squeezed her eyes shut, sliding the folders across the desk. "Did any of the other clients call this morning while I was at court? The other co-defendants who signed retainers?"

Ella shook her head. "No, I imagine they might not unless they get pulled in for questioning." She chewed her lip, brow furrowed, scanning the pages of a file with her index finger, flicking past every color-coded tab she'd placed there herself. "Who must they have as a key witness?" she asked. "Ed Link can't be hinging an entire case on one half-burnt vial of Nether, not to this extent."

"I'm not sure," Sadie admitted. "I intend to find out." She hummed at the back of her throat, gristly and atonal, the sounds of home, with music that would sound alien and frightening to most in the human realm. "We don't want this to go to trial. I cannot allow Astrid to testify on her own behalf. Barring that, her defense is unfortunately rather weak, and I worry they would charge her with perjury." She opened and closed a file cabinet drawer, the emptiness within reminding her that the VCPD still held her notes. "Or taxes. It's not uncommon for that to be someone's downfall, either."

"You'll figure something out," Ella offered, leaning forward to close the drawer. "You always do. That's why you're Sadie Sinclair."

The door opened and closed with a click, the bells Ella had tied to the top jingling quietly. "Hey there, Ms. Sinclair," came a familiar throaty voice, clear but defined.

Sadie stood, bracing herself against the desk in preparation. "Clem," she replied, inviting her in with a wave. "What are you doing here?"

"I dunno, thought you might need my help," she replied, depositing herself into the chair across, eyeing up Ella with a suspicious stare. "I heard Vane is still refusing to be specific on the stand."

"As her attorney, I advised against doing anything more than the bare minimum," Sadie answered. "It opens the door to far too many questions." She sat back in her chair, scooting it closer to the desk. "What kind of help are you offering?"

"Why, are you asking?" Clem pressed. "You have to say please, Ms. Sinclair."

Ella cast a furtive glance between the two, brow furrowed just for a second.

"I'm not here to engage with your petty little power plays, Clem," Sadie replied. "You can either help, or you can find your way out. I assume you remember where the door is located?" She folded her hands atop her desk, giving Clem a hard, dead stare.

A smile toyed with the apples of Clem's cheeks, rosy from the cold and mischievous from her generally irritating nature. "I know who the prosecution's star witness is," she said evenly.

"If you know that from Ed, you absolutely cannot tell me."

"Ed never tells me anything unless he wants something," Clem replied. "I found out because I talked to the rest of the staff at the Sphinx." Clem slid a notepad across the varnished wood with one finger, flipped open to a page scribbled with notes. "This is everything you need."

Sadie squinted at the characters, each of them swimming in front of her vision. "I can't read your writing. I don't think *anyone* can read your writing."

"Then say please, and I'll translate." Clem raised an eyebrow in challenge, waiting for Sadie to acquiesce.

Ella cleared her throat in a perfunctory but obvious way, catching Sadie's stare only for a second. "Should I leave, Say?"

"Should she, Say?" Clem pressed, leaning forward in her chair, her overcoat unbuttoned and flowing over the sides of the chair, revealing the charcoal tweed trousers and white blouse beneath. "I don't know what kind of relationship you have with your secretaries."

"Paralegal," Sadie corrected. "Soon, anyway." She toyed with the buttons on her cuffs, evaluating the situation. "Ella should stay, she has a strong working knowledge of this case." Aside from it being the truth, Sadie was also hesitant to be alone with Clem again. "She has valuable insight."

Clem nodded, sitting back and resting one ankle against the opposite knee. "That's fair, Ms. Sinclair, I understand entirely. Paralegals are a valuable part of any legal team." She pointed at the notepad, and then tapped the edge of it with the eraser end of a pencil. "Happy to help, all you have to do is ask."

"Please," Sadie said, resenting it. "I would be very interested to know what you've found, Clem."

"Excellent." Clem pointed at the top line, a scribble that could either be a name or a bus route, it was hard to tell the numbers from the letters. "They're trying to flip George Dawson, one of the bouncers. He—"

"Two children, family court," Sadie supplied. "I know that much."

Clem raised an appreciative eyebrow and nodded. "Moving on, then. The VCPD is putting a lot of pressure on him because they know it's going to work. They're already prepping him for trial in two days because they're going to promise to drop the charges if he testifies against Astrid."

"What does he know?" Ella asked.

"Does it matter?" Clem retorted with an exaggerated shrug. "He'll say whatever he has to to get rid of this, especially when his lawyer didn't even get him bail." She winked across the desk, and it was simultaneously an outrage and an interest, which lay in Sadie's bones like lead, predictably.

"Thanks to your husband, I think you mean," Sadie corrected. "He's the one that fought bail so hard."

"Regardless, George Dawson is the problem we have to solve. Without him, they don't have enough to convict Astrid of distribution. They barely even have enough to get her for possession, given how many of her staff have access to that basement, and the age of the Nether. That vial was probably down there for six weeks or more." Clem flipped a page, pointing to another line. "This here is the name of George Dawson's caseworker for this family court case."

"How did you get that?" Sadie asked.

Clem shrugged. "I have friends in records."

"How does the caseworker help us?" Sadie knew Clem wouldn't present it unless it was a sure thing, and the smug attitude was rolling off of her in waves. "Please."

"We get the caseworker to back off of George Dawson, grant him custody. The mother used to have it, but her new fella is a known entity in the underworld. Dawson found out and he's been fighting for custody ever since. Poor guy has only been at the Sphinx for a few months. He had a rough time of it when his kids were little."

Sadie nodded, sliding a file across to Clem. "We discovered that he had a few old arrests on his record, but no convictions. His attorney for this case had the strategy to show that he was a changed man with no recent arrests, character witnesses, and a county visit to his living space where he had prepared rooms for his children." She waited for Clem to look through the files, and then took the folder back, closing it. "So, the caseworker?"

"She's been gambling," Clem crowed, triumphant. "And not just that, but running basement games uptown. She's made a tidy little sum."

Ella frowned, leaning back against the door. "And you know that because… ?"

"It's not hard to realize something is off when a family court caseworker is living on the north side alone without inheritance," Clem retorted. "Those salaries wouldn't even cover the rent on a place like that. I knew she was hiding something." She flipped another page, pointing to the final unintelligible scribble. "I encouraged her to grant George custody, not just because he's clearly the more fit parent, given who the mother has taken up with, but because I'm aware of what she's been up to." Clem raised an eyebrow. "What do you think?"

Sadie frowned, preferring to settle things in court, but realizing that for George Dawson, this was likely the best outcome. "I think that's certainly a start."

\#

Chapter Twenty-Four

"Mr. Link, where is your witness?" Judge Liesse asked, stacking files noisily against her desk, impatient and dusted lightly with irritation. "You promised that this case wouldn't waste the court's time."

Ed cleared his throat, stumbling over his words and catching his foot on the leg of the prosecution table. "Deepest apologies, Your Honor," he began, shuffling the note cards in his hands. "I can assure you, our star witness is on the way, but in the meantime, perhaps we can start with the other evidence present. First, we have tax records from the past three years for the Sphinx, which seem to indicate—"

"If you have concerns about tax evasion, I suggest you discuss that with the Internal Revenue Service," the judge interrupted. "You promised me during the bail hearings that you would produce evidence to support holding three suspects and witnesses. Are you currently able to do so?"

"We are, Your Honor," he replied confidently, the greyish sunbeams casting a strange pallor across his face. "We have signed affidavits from four other previous employees that these three suspects were involved in the supply and distribution of Nether."

"Objection," Sadie interrupted, standing from her chair. "Your Honor, these affidavits were procured from previous employees who were fired, for cause I might add, and so shouldn't be admitted into the record. Their testimony is prejudicial to an immense degree." She crossed in front of the table, handing a folder to the judge. "In there, you will find performance reviews for all of these dismissed ex-employees, along with notes of their grievances with their coworkers."

Judge Liesse's frown deepened as she flicked through the pages before she handed it back. "Mr. Link, I am inclined to sustain Ms. Sinclair's objection. Do you have anything else to suggest these people were involved with supply and distribution?"

"Is that your official ruling, Your Honor?" he asked. He was challenging her, angry that his sure-thing case was quickly disintegrating into nothingness. "I'd like an official ruling preserved for the record."

"Sustained," Judge Liesse barked, staring him down. "What else do you have, sir?"

"We have Nether found on the scene," he said, producing grainy black and white photographs of the almost totally inert vial with a proud flourish. "Found in the basement of the Sphinx, the same location as a suspected large-scale drop."

Sadie laughed, letting the sound bounce from her lips with lightness.

"We have an expert witness," he said, brandishing a form. "She's here, Your Honor."

Judge Liesse made a soft tutting noise in her throat. "Very well. Continue."

When the witness was in place, Ed approached the podium, notes in hand. "Good morning, Mrs. Bayer. Thank you for being here in court today, your dedication to Verdance's safety is truly admirable." He leaned against the podium, reading from an unlined card. "Is it your professional, forensic opinion that this is indeed a vial of Nether, a controlled substance not just in this state, but this nation?"

Mrs. Bayer nodded. "Yes, Mr. Link. It is without a doubt, a vial of Nether."

"And what properties does it share with other vials recovered in recent memory?" he asked. "From other crime scenes, other contraband busts, you get the idea."

"My testing suggested that this is part of the stronger batches that started appearing about four months ago," Mrs. Bayer explained. "This Nether tends to be stronger than what we've seen before, from deeper in the Rift. It can be more deadly to mythics and mortals alike, and may or may not show physical signs of use. For example, a quarter of those who use this new Nether don't have purple tinges around the eyes and mouth as we might usually see. This, of course, has led to an explosion of use, especially with young professionals.”

Ed smiled, almost flirting with her. “So it’s your stance that this Nether came from a professional distributor?” he prompted. “It’s much too potent to just be the standard street Nether we’ve seen in past years?”

“Yes,” Mrs. Bayer agreed. “This is much more pure, without any alterations or additives. In some cases, the street-level drug is cut with something else that’s cheaper. Occasionally it enhances the experiences. Sometimes, it kills people.”

“So this Nether specifically is more dangerous?” Ed asked. “Mythics, mortals, they may not know their limits with this new stuff?”

“You’d have to ask the coroner about death rates,” Mrs. Bayer answered. “But yes, from what I’ve seen, that’s accurate.”

“No further questions,” Ed said, flashing Sadie a mocking smirk as he passed her table.

“Mrs. Bayer, thank you so much for being here,” Sadie began, splitting the difference between her desk and the judge’s bench. “I only have a couple of easy questions for you, if you don’t mind.”

“No, of course not. Please, go ahead,” Mrs. Bayer encouraged.

“Does Nether decay?” Sadie asked simply.

Mrs. Bayer shifted uncomfortably in her seat, the wood creaking in protest. “Yes,” she said carefully, looking over Sadie’s shoulder at Ed.

“Did Ed Link tell you not to offer that up unless asked?” Sadie asked. “Actually, withdrawn, I’m sorry, Your Honor. It’s not my intention to impune the integrity of the prosecution or the State’s Attorney.” She turned back to the witness. “Can you please explain, in your expert opinion, what you mean by decay?”

“It loses potency over time,” Mrs. Bayer said with a fair amount of trepidation. “The fresher the Nether is from the Rift, the stronger the properties.”

“And how old would you say the vial discovered in the basement of the Sphinx was?” Sadie questioned, pretending to go over her notes so as not to seem too aggressive. Juries hated an aggressive attorney, especially if she was a woman.

Mrs. Bayer gave a soft, sad sigh. "I would guess at least six weeks, perhaps eight."

"Would a vial of that age cause a patron or an employee to become inebriated? Would it increase a shifter's strength, or a seer's visions?" Sadie asked innocently, as though she didn't already know the answer from half a dozen other cases.

"It's unlikely it would have a strong effect," the witness answered.

"And, in your professional opinion, is it possible that a customer or a previous employee of the Sphinx may have, in the preceding six to eight weeks, hidden a vial in the basement for themselves?"

Ed nearly knocked over his chair as he stood. "Objection!" he shouted. "Beyond the scope, Your Honor, Mrs. Bayer is a forensic expert, not a detective."

"Withdrawn," Sadie said with a smile, flashing polite teeth at the jury. It had been enough to let them know what she'd planned they should, that there was an ocean of reasonable doubt as to whose the vial was. "Apologies, Mrs. Bayer, and thank you for your candor. No more questions, Your Honor, the witness can be released."

Judge Liesse nodded, waiting for the witness to exit the podium. "Mr. Link, your witness?" she prompted.

Another junior lawyer from the State's Attorney's office rushed in through the huge, carved wooden doors, frantic and empty-handed. Sadie recognized him from the gala, young, unsure, and a little wobbly on his state law. He whispered into Ed's ear, and before he even stepped away, Ed's face reddened with rage, crawling up over his starched collar.

"It would seem that our witness has decided not to testify," he said evenly, the boiling anger roiling just below the surface. "But we would ask for a recess to sort this out, Your Honor. I'm not sure he quite understands what's at stake here."

"Counselors, meet me in chambers," Judge Liesse spat, not even waiting for them to reply, simply disappearing through the door with a swirl of her robes.

Sadie collected her files, tucking them under her arm as she laid a reassuring arm on Astrid's shoulder. It was good for the jury to see her look vulnerable, especially if she had to take the targeted mythic defense. She'd already hinted at it in her opening statement that morning.

"What did you do this time, Sinclair?" Ed spat at her the moment they were in the corridor. "Tampering with witnesses again? Falsifying evidence? I'll have your license for this, you up-jumped—"

"Your case is weak, sir," Sadie shot back, walking straight ahead, not even gracing him with the courtesy of a dirty look. "And perhaps the next time you send your wife to sleep with me to garner information, please be sure that it's not quite so blatantly obvious." She breezed past him, opening the door to the judge's chambers.

"Good, you're both here," Judge Liesse said brusquely. "Mr. Link, you assured me that you would have this witness in place. What is your strategy here?"

Ed fumbled with his briefcase, still staring at Sadie with wide, horrified eyes. "I, uh..." he trailed off, smacking the corner against a chair. "Apologies, Your Honor, this has all caught me a bit off-guard."

"From where I'm sitting, which is the important viewpoint here, Mr. Link, it looks a lot like the VCPD is working with the State's Attorney's office to stitch up an entrepreneur of the community." Judge Liesse stared at him over her desk, the fabric of her robes flowing over the sides of her chair. "They have continually served warrants throughout this entire process, desperate for more evidence to shore up this case. All they have managed to find is one vial of impotent Nether." She checked her notes, frowning. "I suppose there are also the three employees that Captain Lindell arrested in the raid, correct?"

Ed unlatched his case, presenting a stack of files. "No, Your Honor, there's also the issue of the taxes, and we have two witnesses that will swear that—"

"No, Mr. Link, that's not going to be good enough to pursue a distribution charge," the judge interrupted. "Do you have anything else?"

"Our witness," he said. "Just a short recess would be enough to—"

"To intimidate him into testifying?" Sadie interjected. "Your Honor, the

VCPD used this man's status in family court against him. He's trying to obtain custody of his children, and Captain Lindell and the rest of her team knew that an arrest would preclude him from doing so."

Judge Liesse's face clouded with anger, and she closed Ed's file with dangerous precision. "Is this true, Mr. Link? Your star witness has an open case in family court?"

"Yes, Your Honor," Ed admitted, sheepish as he gathered up his dismissed files. "But that has no bearing on—"

"Mr. Link, this is a reprehensible manipulation of the law," Judge Liesse spat. "You can have your recess, sir, but it's for me to decide if I'm declaring a mistrial. Get out of my chambers, both of you." She pointed at Sadie with a fountain pen, ink dripping from the nib. "I was rooting for you, Ms. Sinclair, but this trick of collating a co-defense of every employee alongside their employer is not how I thought you would have proceeded in this case." She shook her head, shooing them both away. "Tomorrow morning, nine o'clock. I can safely say I will be dismissing this case with prejudice, Mr. Link, and you can tell your boss, the Mr. State's Attorney, to stop wasting my time with mythic hunts and get back to controlling the crews in this city."

\#

"Hey." Clem emerged from the shadows, her hands shoved deep into her pockets to keep out the encroaching cold.

"I didn't expect to see you here," Sadie said, pausing in the alley, keys in her hands. "I thought you'd be halfway to the border by now, ready to spend your paycheck on a vacation somewhere warmer than here.

"I'm not much for beaches." Clem tilted her head, the night's weight creating deep lines across her face. "I heard things went your way in court today."

"I can't complain." She didn't want to ask how Clem knew that, because really, she already knew the answer. "We could have avoided trial if we had secured some better information earlier on in the case, however."

"Hmm." Clem stepped closer, bracing a hand against the wall, her fingers elegantly arched. "You know, Ms. Sinclair, I think I could do a better job the second time around."

Sadie raised an eyebrow, tucking her hair tightly against her ears. "The case is all but over, you know. The judge is going to declare a mistrial."

"That's not quite what I meant." The night air blew in around them both, teasing at the hems of their coats before dislodging a flier down the alley. The faded, illegible page rustled further away, tumbling into the street.

"Then what did you mean?"

"I don't like to leave a job unfinished." Clem stretched out a hand, brushing first against Sadie's chin and dragging upwards, her fingertips light but sure.

Sadie caught her by the wrist, leaning forward off the brick. The wool of her coat tore away from the rough clay, the sound of it lost amid the whistled draft that pooled around their ankles. "So finish it, then."

Her eyes were already closed when their lips met, an inviting, sumptuous warmth pressing back against the biting cold. Clem's hands drifted to her waist, lingering there, grasping through the layers of thick wool. "I live upstairs," Sadie managed to get out between increasingly fervent kisses.

Clem dragged her through the door and up the stairwell, stopping every third step to kiss her again, not letting either of them deepen it until they were at Sadie's door.

The hinge snapped shut with a loud click and she was fumbling against the wall for the light switch. "Don't," Clem whispered. "You look too perfect in the moonlight."

The bluish-grey glow flooded the rug and the hardwood flooring, engulfing them both and cresting over the evening shadows laid across their faces. Coats fell to the floor in a heap, heels kicked into the corner as Sadie led them both to her bedroom, past perfectly leveled art hung in the hallway.

Clem released the buttons of Sadie's shirt one at a time, slowing her pace and opening her mouth, letting loose a small groan of anticipation. "Sadie Sinclair, I don't know who you were thinking about last time, but I will be shadows-damned if it's not me, this time."

Sadie didn't bother arguing or trying to correct her. Instead, she focused on the firm smoothness of Clem's collarbone, pressing back against her fingertips. She kissed along one side and then the other, enjoying the sensation for the first time in years. Ella was a foregone conclusion. Clem, on the other hand, was a terrible plan, but the way her breath was catching in her throat was enough to make Sadie forget all of that.

She unbuttoned Clem's shirt, throwing it to the floor, unhooking her bra, and feeling soft flesh under her hands and tightness pulling between her thighs and it was a rush of heady, foolish, brilliantly, blindingly bad ideas all at once that were too tempting to ignore.

Scales flashed in the moonlight, dusted across Clem's legs, crawling up one side and dripping down the other. "You're a shifter," Sadie breathed.

"Don't spread that around," Clem replied, breaking away from kissing Sadie's neck just for a moment. "It's why I helped you, Sinclair. I don't want to be targeted, and that's the way things are going in Verdance lately." She kissed Sadie full on the mouth, sliding her tongue into her mouth and removing the rest of Sadie's clothes until they were both bare, pressed against each other on the bed, tangled in sheets and their chests heaving with the effort.

Sadie didn't even try to resist the cliff-face when it rose up to meet her, pulling up from the floor and pushing her over the edge, her cries muffled in Clem's shoulder. She was left gasping for breath, spread out on the pillows like a feast. "I think you finished the job," she managed to whisper, laughing as she covered her face.

"Good," Clem replied, tossing her a husky laugh. "My honor remains intact."

\#

Chapter Twenty-Five

Sadie pushed through her office door after court the next morning, bolstered by the mistrial, the inability for the prosecution to refile that motion, and the heady feeling of having been wanted, and had, and given a furtive kiss goodbye as Clem left the night before.

"Morning," Ella said, giving her a strange look. "How was court?"

"The judge declared a mistrial," Sadie announced proudly. "Astrid is thrilled, of course. She'll have to be very careful going forward, because I don't think that Captain Lindell is going to let this go. Thank you for all your work, Ella, and I mean that."

Ella nodded. "Of course, Say. It's my job."

"Is everything alright?" Sadie asked, hanging her coat on the rack. "You seem distracted."

"You never told me you had a preference for women," Ella said evenly, busying herself with paperwork. "We've worked together for years, and you never mentioned it."

"Oh," Sadie trailed off, refusing to look over at her. "Where did you get that idea from?"

"Clementine Dorefield," Ella replied. "She was practically ready to climb over your desk yesterday, by the looks of it. *Say please, Ms. Sinclair,*" she echoed in a mocking tone. Ella rolled her eyes, snorting a laugh.

"I didn't think you'd understand."

Ella glanced at her. "I'm not naive, Say," she said acerbically, the hint of sarcasm lightening her tone. "A letter came for you, by the way." She gestured vaguely at the desk, a silvery envelope askew atop the leather writing pad.

Sadie stared, unsure of what to make of the delivery. She had never anticipated contact from home, not with how everything had turned out. They had promised her peace in the human realm, so long as she went quietly.

"Everything okay?" Ella asked, turned towards the filing cabinet as she organized the newly redacted court documents.

"Yes," Sadie trailed off, staring as she turned over the envelope to reveal the iridescent wax seal on the other side, pressed with her aunt's coat of arms and embossed with shimmer. "I mean, no. Yes."

"Say?" Ella prompted, peering into the office. "Who's it from?"

"Oh, it's just a gala invitation for next month, but I don't think I'll go," Sadie lied. "I'm sorry, Ella, I just need a moment to collect my thoughts after court." For the first time ever, she closed her office door on Ella and sank back into her chair just before her legs gave out.

The parchment was folded with sharp, crisp creases, the calligraphy impeccable with every articulate swirl.

My liege,

I have spent these past days trying to locate you in the Human Realm. I fear time has already passed for you there, and you will have thought we had forgotten about who the rightful ruler is.

We have not.

There are a number of us who question both the prophecy's interpretation and the court's verdict, as well as your aunt's ascendency to the throne. I have included a portion of birch tea, no doubt you will be in need of it, and a mirror to our realm. It will only reach me, so you may contact me in confidence.

I have taken steps to conceal this letter in its journey, but please know, your aunt is watching. Sending written correspondence is not safe.

Ever your faithful servant and friend,

Florian

Sadie tilted her head as she examined each of the letters in their stead. The paper glowed bright in the mirror, sealed with Fae reagents. The pink–purple haze reflected back onto her face, an unpleasant reminder of her exile. Already, the tear between what was and what may yet come to pass began to grow, fraying each thread of possibility at the edges. She ran her fingers over the gilded edges of the mirror, wishing she could contact him right that moment. She pulled away, sliding the pouch of tea into her drawer. No.

If she was to ensure his safety, she had to exercise caution to the highest degree. Her aunt was dangerous, as were those who supported her. Sadie's neck flushed with the heat of unbridled anxiety as it crept through her every sense. Whatever was going on at home, it was likely to spill Fae and human blood alike.

* * *

End of Exiled Advocate

Keep reading for a sneak peek of the next book in The Ruptured Realms Universe: Clocktower Elegy, exhibit B in The Vane Dossier.

Want to get sneak peeks, exclusive sales, and free books? Join the newsletter at Linktr.ee/RyannFletcherWrites

Enter The Ruptured Realms Universe

The Ruptured Realms encompasses three different series, with three different main characters. Read them in linear order:

1. Rhapsody in Flames (The Vane Dossier, exhibit A)
2. Exiled Advocate (Sadie Sinclair, Esquire: book one)
3. Clocktower Elegy (The Vane Dossier, exhibit B)
4. Séamus Carlucci: new series coming soon

The Ruptured Realms will contain twelve novels across these three series! Sign up for the newsletter at Linktr.ee/RyannFletcherWrites for access to beta reader signups, advanced reader copy giveaways, and sneak peeks.

Preview for Clocktower Elegy (The Vane Dossier: exhibit B)

Bright sunlight, humid and oppressive, beat down from the sky, drawing a bead of sweat from her forehead that she magnanimously allowed to slide over sharp cheekbones, falling to drip down onto her collar. Summer in Verdance had arrived, and while heat was a sensible vacation from the freezing temperatures of winter, in the city, it was out of the icebox, into the frying pan.

"Ginnie?" Arthur prompted, his stare boring into her the same way it had for the past six shadows-damned months. "Did you hear what I just said?"

"Yeah," Virginia lied, popping the joints in her fingers just to feel the light pain of relief. "Homicide."

"I never said it was homicide. We haven't confirmed either way." He leaned in closer, so much so that she had to resist the overwhelming urge to jerk away from him. "Did you know that it's homicide because of your seeing?" he whispered.

She took three steps backwards, nearly colliding with the coroner. "Sorry," she muttered, straightening to adjust the twisted strap of her left suspender. "No, Arthur, that's not why. I have eyes, don't I? It's obvious that he didn't do this himself. There's no way that distributor overdosed. He'd know what human limits were better than anyone, even with this new potent stuff cropping up in the city."

"That was my thought, too." Arthur waved several detectives into the room, watching as they observed the body. Approximately six-foot-one, broad shouldered, built like a brick shithouse, it was Merv Knuckles, a known member of the Kraken crew who'd worked his way up from being an enforcer.

He was on his back, purple-tinged eyes wide as he stared up at the ceiling, the bleached bed sheets pulled up to his shoulders and topped with a light grey feather quilt. "If we can't get a lid on this, the feds are going to be all over it." He turned, answering some baseline question that the photographer had about the scene. "They're looking for any reason to get overly involved with our cases. That new anti-terrorism Nether law means they have all kinds of jurisdictional seniority over the VCPD that they didn't before."

"I'm not with the VCPD, so I fail to see how this is my problem," Virginia retorted. She tilted her head, examining the scene. "No signs of forced entry," she said. "No signs of a struggle, either."

"Everything points to an accidental overdose, Ginnie," he replied. "Except for the fact that he would have known."

"Suicide?" she asked. "Although, I can't imagine kicking my own bucket if I was running half the city's Nether rings, and living in a place as nice as this one." She gently tugged the blanket down after the photographer had finished, turning over the victim's hand. "No visible defensive wounds, as far as I can see." She pulled it down further, grimacing. "Naked."

Arthur picked at the badge on his arm, the tiny metallic clasps inaudible against the din of the investigation. "I need your help." He sighed, writing something in the margins of the notepad he had pulled from his pants pocket.

"Just say whatever it is you have to say, Arthur, I don't have all shadows-damned day." Virginia folded the blanket down over the bedsheet, leaving the corpse for the coroner. "Out with it, Dixon."

"You haven't been at headquarters much recently."

"And?"

He watched her, moving aside for the additional detectives to exit. "And as a consultant, I would have thought you would consult more." He straightened after they left, the weight of his position already taking a toll in the lightly greying five'oclock shadow that fanned out across his jawline. "Especially after learning what you did at that compound." He turned, staring, the same way he'd been staring at her for months, as if he expected her to look any different than she always had.

Virginia's jaw clamped, her teeth grinding with the indecision. She hadn't told Arthur that she'd been unable to access those abilities again after the raid, and she didn't want to, either. She didn't want to discuss it at all. "I've been busy with clients."

"More missing mythics? Because you know, they really should be reported to the VCPD for—"

"No," she interrupted. "Minor financial crimes. An inheritance, some fraud, a huckster here or there. You know, the kind of stuff the VCPD can't be bothered with."

"That hardly sounds like a full schedule, Ginnie," he replied. "And if I know you, then those cases aren't scratching that itch."

"It's better than almost dying twice in ten days," she shot back. He was right, but she'd never admit it. Virginia dusted along the metal bed frame, hoping for usable prints, but finding none. "It's perfectly respectable work."

"I just thought you'd be reaching for more challenging cases." Arthur was testing her, and they both knew it, but instead of pushing further, he gestured towards the snag in the carpet amid flattened fibers. "What do you think?" he asked.

"I think that no matter what you find here, the feds are going to stick their paws into it." Virginia pushed past the door and down the steps, hunting for any sign that the victim had fought back. "Whoever dragged him up the stairs, it was someone strong."

He nodded, still watching. "Nothing for sure?"

"He was probably dead already," she replied. "Either that, or unconscious. It's plausible, given how much Nether must have been in his system." Virginia inspected three nearly invisible droplets gathered on the stairs, likely old stains. They definitely weren't blood. "Assuming it's a crew hit, do you have any leads?"

"None," he replied, shaking his head. "None of the usual suspects are talking."

"No connections?"

"None that we can find." Arthur stood just over her shoulder, examining the droplets. "But I thought that you might see something that we hadn't."

Virginia turned, brushing him off. "You don't have to hover, you know."

"It would just be very advantageous if we—"

"There's that word again, we." She ducked under his arm and reached for the arm of the dust-covered cash register, setting the drawer open with a dull chime of the half-hearted bell. "There is no we." She rifled through the drawer before slamming it closed again. "No cash. Pity."

"It would just go into evidence, anyway."

"Obviously, Arthur." She allowed herself a private roll of her eyes before she turned back to face him. "Could there have been any witnesses? Neighbors, maybe? Or a gardener?"

"I asked around, but nothing. The bedroom window is blocked by the scaffolding of the neighbor building an extension next door. Shouldn't have been allowed, but Eugenia Patten on the council signed off on it." Arthur followed her into the back room, leaning against the door frame with one shoulder. "It's a shame we couldn't put her away for those documents."

"She's got enough lawyers to get out of anything," Virginia retorted. She was growing tired of his shadow, preferring to work alone, given the opportunity. She reached out, brushing her fingertips against the desk drawer's handle, but nothing came. "I'm not surprised you didn't nab her."

"Do you sense anything?" he asked.

"I don't know, do you?" she shot back. "You're the sheriff, maybe you could deduce something for once."

"And you're a—" he stopped himself, moving closer in the room and reducing his voice to a whisper. "A seer, Ginnie."

"It doesn't work like that." She avoided him again, crossing the corridor into the kitchen. The marble counter tops were spotless, no doubt scrubbed by an underpaid cleaner. "Sends a message, doesn't it? Killing him at home?"

"I was ruminating on that, too."

"Turf war?" Virginia asked, leaning against the smooth, unmarred surface. "Competitor moving into the area?"

"Not impossible," Arthur agreed. "It would be helpful to get a clearer reading."

"It's difficult when you're following me around." She dodged him again, circling the wood island in the center of the kitchen to prod at several untouched, sharpened kitchen knives. "If I could just call it up like that, I would."

"Can't you?" he asked.

Virginia barely repressed a sigh and a snide remark. "Obviously not. If I could, don't you think I would have known a little sooner?"

He peered out the kitchen door, waving an officer down the corridor towards the back entrance. "Have you used it at all since the raid?"

The question hung in the air thicker than the encroaching scent of death and decay. "I have to get to an appointment," she replied, choosing to ignore it entirely. "I'm already running late and midday traffic downtown is a shadows-damned nightmare."

"Ginnie."

"Arthur."

He hesitated, running a hand over his bald head, shiny with the glisten of sweat. "You haven't, have you?"

"It doesn't matter. Maybe it was one too many hits to the skull. Maybe I imagined the whole thing," she sniped. "I told you, I have to get to the office. My office."

"Jo said it was pretty stark, what happened then. Ursa's apartment, then Fiske's compound." Arthur exhaled unevenly, unsure. "Whatever this is, seeing or... or something else, you should try to figure it out. I'm worried about you, Ginnie."

The words sparked through her chest like lightning, destructive and devastating. She drew in a breath and held it, trying to convince herself that punching him in the jaw wasn't in her best interest, and neither was sprinting away from the scene. "I'm pretty sure you lost that privilege a long time ago."

"Wasn't it you who said we were friends once? Why not try to get back there?" he asked gently, too gently, giving her a look of pity that roiled in her gut.

"Now isn't the time for this," she replied gruffly, pushing past him into the immaculate living room. "I have work to do, and so do you."

He grabbed her gently by the elbow, pulling her closer so that he could whisper. "Ginnie, the feds picked up three ex-Ruby Thorn enforcers last week, and they're singing louder than canaries in a coal mine about an inferno witch causing a lot of damage last winter."

"Shit," Virginia grumbled, allowing him to stop her. "Did they know Jolie's name?"

"They knew enough to have feds asking me why I didn't follow up on tips about an unregistered fire demon last winter." Arthur gave her a sideways glance, half squinted in the overbearing sunlight filtering through the large bay window. "They heard enough to know that's what she is, regardless of what the enforcers thought. They'd give her up in a heartbeat if it meant a reduced sentence for themselves. I have to tell the feds something at some point, and I think it would be better if neither of you were in the city."

"I'll think about it." She picked up an expensive, empty vase, blown glass and shimmering. It probably cost more than her yearly salary. "I have to go."

Arthur didn't reach for her again, knowing better than to make her stay. "I thought we could grab coffee with Captain Lindell, really dig into the meat of these deaths," he offered, adjusting the silver belt buckle that matched the badge on his arm.

"I don't need coffee to pass off my notes." Virginia stepped through the front door, squinting at the assault of the afternoon sun. "I've got too many cases on my docket for that."

"You know, I had hoped that by working together on the Fiske thing, you two would at least grow into a professional respect." He eyed her again, and she was so tired of being so exposed, so seen, especially by him.

"Take it up with her."

"Is something going on with Lindell, Ginnie?" Arthur was at her shoulder now, asking her in a muted, overly calm tone.

Virginia barked out a laugh. "No."

"I just wondered, seeing as you've been avoiding the station."

"I already told you, I've been busy." She waved at the up-and-coming north side neighborhood, one more sign of just how much Verdance was changing. "You should make yourself busy with this overdose, or homicide, whatever it is." She shrugged dismissively. "I'd be making it my top priority, if it was me."

"Sheriff Dixon, the coroner needed to speak to you," one of the detectives said. She flashed a smile at Virginia, who decided to pretend that hadn't happened.

"Sure," he replied with a curt nod. "Ginnie, I'll give you a call at the office if anything jumps."

"Call the apartment if it's past five. Jolie will at least be there, she can take a message." Virginia strode away, regretting having picked up the phone that morning. Another mysterious death, feds, and shadows-damned Arthur to deal with. The only thing that would make it worse was having to deal with Shirin, too.

"Vane!"

Virginia groaned and kept walking. If she was quick, she'd make it to her car with plausible deniability that she'd heard anything in the first place. Her fingers were on the handle, almost an escape, when Lindell caught up with her.

"Hey," Captain Shirin Lindell said, pressing a hand against the car door. "Didn't you hear me?"

"I have a lot on my mind."

"If I'd have known you'd be here, I would have—"

"Would have what?" Virginia interrupted. "Called the feds to let them know they'd have jurisdiction?"

Shirin pressed harder against the door, her bicep flexing beneath the crisp white of her uniform shirt. "No, I would have shortened my shift to make sure I didn't miss you. You've been a hard woman to get hold of."

"You need to relax," Virginia hissed, wrenching the car door open anyways, the hinge creaking with protest. "Arthur already suspects something is going on."

"Why, did he say something?"

"Yes." Virginia climbed into the car, shoving the key into the ignition. "And this isn't a conversation I want to have at a crime scene." She settled into the seat, ready to drive the moment she had the opportunity. "My guess is a homicide, he pissed off the wrong undesirable." She nodded towards the bakery as her car's engine rumbled quietly. "Look for yourself."

"Not just plain old overdose, then?"

"Did you really think we'd get that lucky?"

Shirin studied her, forearms rested against the door despite the heat and the black metal of the car. "No, I suppose not, but it's not as if overdoses are uncommon these days."

"It's homicide, Shirin. A crew hit job, one more for the books. Tell the family to contact his life insurance company, and let's call it a day." Virginia slid the car into gear, easing forward enough to get Shirin to release her grip on the door. "I'll see you around."

She pulled off the driveway and back onto the road, the suspension or something else rattling underneath. She turned left, towards her apartment. It was almost lunch time, and she hadn't left anything for the kid to eat.

About the Author

Ryann Fletcher is a writer who lives in Glasgow with too many books and craft supplies. She writes science fiction and fantasy novels because real life is boring without spaceships and magic. She loves to cook and go for long hikes in the wilderness, searching for the meaning of life and probably the keys she lost three days ago.

You can connect with me on:

🌐 https://ryannfletcher.com

📘 https://facebook.com/RyannFletcherWrites

🔗 https://instagram.com/RyannFletcherWrites

🔗 https://www.tiktok.com/@ryannfletcherwrites

🔗 https://patreon.com/RyannFletcherWrites

Subscribe to my newsletter:

✉ https://linktr.ee/ryannfletcherwrites